The
Princess School

Who's the Fairest?

The Princess School

Who's the Fairest?

Jane B. Mason ✷ Sarah Hines Stephens

SCHOLASTIC INC.

New York Toronto London Auckland Sydney
Mexico City New Delhi Hong Kong Buenos Aires

Copyright © 2004 by Jane B. Mason and Sarah Hines Stephens.

All rights reserved.
Published by Scholastic Inc.
SCHOLASTIC and associated logos are trademarks
and/or registered trademarks of Scholastic Inc.

ISBN 0-439-56553-7

12 11 10 9 8 7 6 5 4 3 2 1   4 5 6 7 8 9/0

Printed in the U.S.A.   40

First printing, March 2004

The
Princess School

Who's the Fairest?

Chapter One
Sleepless Beauty

"Pass the oatmeal," said a growly voice at the end of the table. It was Gruff, the crankiest of Snow White's seven surrogate fathers. His bushy eyebrows met in the middle of his forehead due to his constant scowl. And he wasn't grumpy just because it was early in the morning. Gruff was cranky *all* the time.

"Achoooo!" Wheezer let out a loud sneeze. Oatmeal flew off his spoon, landing with a splat on Nod's face. Nod, who had been drifting off to sleep, sat up straight and elbowed Gruff in the side.

"Er, please," Gruff added.

But at the other end of the long, low table, ten-year-old Snow White stared blankly into her bowl of already-cold hot cereal.

"Snow White," Mort said gently. Though he was barely as tall as the table they were eating at, Mort was

1

essentially the dwarf in charge and happened to be sitting next to Snow. He put his small, pudgy hand on her pale-skinned arm. "Dear, is everything all right?"

Snow White looked up to see seven pairs of friendly but worried eyes staring at her.

"Is everything okay?" echoed Hap. He had a smile on his face like he always did, but his typically easygoing expression was full of concern.

Snow tried her best to smile back. "Oh, yes," she replied. "I'm just fine." She reached for the large spoon in the cast-iron pot of oatmeal. "Who wants seconds?" she asked.

Nearly all of the dwarves raised their colorful ceramic bowls in the air. "I do, I do!" they chorused, pounding their wooden spoons on the table in a musical rhythm. Then they began to sing merrily:

> More oatmeal, more for me,
> More for my tummy, yes, indeed.
> Fill my bowl up to the top,
> I'll eat and eat and never stop!

Snow couldn't help but smile at the little men who had become her family. Their woodland cottage was always full of laughter and music, and Snow loved it. But even the dwarves' silly breakfast song couldn't make Snow forget her troubles that morning. As she refilled their bowls with steaming-hot oatmeal, she forced herself to hum a few bars of the cereal song. The last thing she wanted was to make the dwarves worry.

After seconds — and thirds for Dim and Hap — the dwarves cleared the table, carrying the dishes to the sink. Then they each took a pail filled with a lunch Snow had prepared (roast venison sandwiches and berry tarts) and hugged her good-bye. After gathering up their shovels, axes, and picks and pulling their rough-spun shirts down over their round bellies, they headed off to the mine.

"Good-bye," Snow called as the dwarves scurried down the path whistling a work song. It was so early that the sun was just rising, but Snow and the dwarves had been up for hours. The woodland cottage was a place for early risers. Every morning the dwarves woke Snow with a rise-and-shine serenade. Then they scampered downstairs to set the table and get the fire going for breakfast.

Snow remembered those mornings when the merry singing would wake her from a peaceful slumber. But lately she'd been wide-awake even before the serenading began. In fact, she'd been up most of the night for almost a week, worrying about the upcoming Maiden

Games at Princess School. And on the few occasions that she'd been able to doze off, she'd had terrible nightmares!

When Meek, the shy dwarf at the end of the line, had disappeared down the forest path, Snow closed the cottage door and headed to the sink to wash the breakfast dishes. As she filled the basin with warm, soapy water, she remembered the Coronation Ball at Princess School just the week before.

Everyone at Princess School had been looking forward to the ball, and it was truly a magical night. Not only did Snow go to the ball with her new friends Briar Rose, Cinderella Brown, and Rapunzel Arugula, Ella had actually been crowned Princess of the Ball! It had been Snow's first ball, and it was better than she'd ever dreamed. There'd been dancing and food and boys from the Charm School . . . everything was perfect.

But then Malodora, her awful stepmother, had appeared onstage to announce the upcoming Maiden Games — the annual competition between Princess School and its archrival, the Grimm School. Grimm was the academy attended by all the young witches in the land, and most of the girls who went there were less than friendly. A prominent figure at the Grimm School, Malodora had come to make the announcement because she herself would be a judge at the Games.

And to scare me, Snow thought. If that was Malodora's intention, it had worked.

Until that night, Snow hadn't laid eyes on her stepmother since she'd run away from home. As she rinsed one of the bowls and set it in the carved wood strainer, she shuddered at the memory of living with Malodora. The woman made snakes and spiders flee in fear.

When Snow's father had first told Snow he was going to remarry, Snow had been ecstatic. Snow's mother had died when Snow was a tiny baby and she had always longed for a motherly figure to share things with and look up to. She'd had high hopes for her relationship with her father's new wife.

When Malodora first arrived at Snow's father's castle, she seemed content to be queen. She had a lovely castle to run and she herself was beautiful to look at. Everyone said so. Even Malodora herself couldn't help but gaze at her own reflection in the large looking glass she'd brought with her to the castle.

Snow liked to sit and gaze with her — until Malodora asked her to leave. "You make me nervous with your staring. Don't you have anything better to do?" the queen had said curtly. Snow had curtsied and left quietly. She'd only wanted to make her new mother feel welcome. But the next time she peeked into Malodora's chambers, hoping to sit with her, the looking glass was gone.

Snow kept trying. She did everything she could think of to please her new stepmother. But instead of warming to Snow, Malodora got colder. She looked at Snow with disapproving stares. The more Snow smiled, the more Malodora frowned. Snow's very presence seemed to make her unhappy.

Malodora began to spend most of her time alone in her attic chamber. Since the chamber was off-limits, nobody was sure what the queen was doing. But the strange lights and harsh smells made Snow suspect that her stepmother was concocting potions and casting spells. Sometimes Snow even heard voices.

The maid told her there was a magic mirror in the attic that Malodora spoke to, asking it questions. The mirror claimed to speak the truth, yet the more Malodora spoke to it, the angrier she grew. "There's something wrong with that looking glass," the maid confided to Snow. "I think it's cracked!"

Then something truly horrible happened. Snow's father disappeared. One evening he sweetly kissed his young daughter good night, and in the morning he was nowhere to be found. When Snow asked her stepmother where he had gone, she simply replied that he'd had to go to sea.

"Why didn't he say good-bye?" Snow had asked, her eyes full of tears.

"Perhaps he didn't think it was necessary," Malodora had replied icily.

Snow wiped her nose on her sleeve as she placed a freshly washed bowl with the others next to the stone sink. It had been so long since she'd seen her father, and whenever she thought of him, it was difficult not to cry.

With her father gone, life in the castle had changed utterly. Snow began to worry. The halls she had once skipped down now appeared dark and scary. The flowers withered in the gardens. Even the once-cozy fires burning in the grates hissed and popped, sending out sparks and frightening Snow away. The castle staff only dared to speak to Snow in whispers. They told her Malodora had taken a job as headmistress at the Grimm School. And in hushed tones they told her, "Beware!"

Snow was so lonely without her father she decided to reach out once more. Perhaps Malodora was lonely, too. Summoning her courage she'd climbed the stairs to her stepmother's attic room carrying a tea tray laden with cookies and pastries. When she reached the top she stopped. She didn't have a free hand to knock, but the door was standing open just a crack. Snow leaned against the door frame and was about to call out when she caught sight of Malodora.

Her stepmother was bent over in front of her mirror, stooped with laughter. Her cackles turned into howls. She was watching an image in the mirror, an image of Snow's father struggling on board a ship in a terrible storm! The image disappeared and a horrible face appeared in the glass. It, too, looked amused.

"Well done, my queen," the mirror said. "Your worthless husband is lost in your spell, sailing the endless sea. May he never see the shore again.

"The castle is nearly yours. Only that ridiculous cheerful child stands in your way."

Shocked by what she was seeing, Snow dropped the tray with a clatter and a hot splash. Malodora had certainly heard her, but Snow did not stop to look back or apologize for the mess. Snow fled the castle that very moment.

It was a terrifying journey. Snow had stumbled along the forest paths, her vision blurred by tears. She did not know where to go or what to do, and she felt completely alone. But when she stumbled upon the little cottage in the woods, it immediately seemed like home.

It was Meek whom Snow White met first — he was outside chopping wood. But he was so shy he wouldn't talk to her! He ran behind the woodpile and peeked timidly through a knothole. Luckily Hap came out to help with the stacking, and he chattered kindly with

Snow, saying nothing about her blotchy, tear-stained cheeks. In an instant Snow felt like they were old friends. Soon the rest of the little men — Wheezer, Mort, Nod, Dim, and Gruff — came out to see what the commotion was about. Gruff took one look at Snow and stormed back inside. The rest of the dwarves welcomed her with open arms. She had supper with them that very night and, after she told the dwarves her tale, they insisted she stay. Snow agreed to spend one night, and had lived in the woodland cottage ever since.

At first Snow had been nervous that her step-mother would come after her. With her sorceress talents and all-seeing mirror, Malodora most certainly knew where Snow was. But for whatever reason, she left Snow alone. Perhaps she was glad to be rid of her. One thing was certain: Snow was glad to be away. In the cottage she felt safe . . . at least until recently.

Ever since her stepmother's appearance at the Princess School ball, Snow couldn't shake the creepy feeling that Malodora was watching her in her awful mirror. . . . Sometimes Snow could swear she felt the sorceress's icy fingers on her neck! And if Snow did anything to draw attention to herself — like compete in the Maiden Games — it might enrage her step-mother. Snow knew that every Princess School student was expected to participate, but she'd have to find a way to get out of it.

Glancing at the carved wooden cuckoo clock, Snow realized that if she didn't hurry she'd be late for school. She grabbed her cape, books, and scrolls and rushed out the door.

Every tree and stone along the path was familiar to Snow, so it was easy to move quickly. The morning air was crisp but not cold, and the sky was cerulean blue. Usually Snow drank in the woodland beauty. Today she barely noticed it.

Stepping into the lane, she immediately spied the shadowy Grimm School. Its smoke-stained spires poked at the sky. Snow resisted the temptation to sample the school's gingerbread gate — doing so was a sure way to be ensnared by the nasty Grimm girls. Snow hurried past so quickly that she forgot to look where she was going and ran — *smack!* — into Lucinta Pintch, a fast-talking snoop of a witch from Grimm.

"What's your hurry?" Lucinta asked, eyeing Snow mischievously. "Care to rest for a spell?" Quick as a flash she raised her twisted black wand toward Snow. "Or are you worried your stepmother might see you showing your face in her territory?"

Snow gasped, horrified by Lucinta's words.

If all of the Grimm witches know I'm Malodora's step-daughter, they must also know she hates me! Snow thought. *The whole school is probably out to get me!*

Swallowing hard, Snow stepped around Lucinta without uttering a word. Up ahead, she could see Rapunzel in the distance. She hurried to catch up to her friend. Behind her, Lucinta's cackling voice echoed on the fall breeze.

Chapter Two
Confidence

When Snow caught up to Rapunzel and Rapunzel's best friend, Prince Valerian, they were deep in conversation.

"We've just got to win the Golden Ball," Rapunzel said, her brown eyes flashing.

Snow knew the Golden Ball was just that — a shimmering orb. But it was also the coveted trophy for the winner of the Maiden Games.

Rapunzel hitched up the skirts of her gown and strode down the path determinedly, as if getting to school first would guarantee her the prize.

"Slow down, princess," Val called to Rapunzel as she leaped over a fallen log and hurried ahead. Then he turned. "Hello, Snow," he said. He smiled charmingly and offered her a hand to get over the fallen tree.

Snow returned the smile and took Val's hand. He really was a nice prince. Snow could see why he was

Rapunzel's best friend. And being with *nice* people was just what Snow needed right now.

Val called out to Rapunzel again. "What's your hurry? The competition isn't for a week!"

Rapunzel turned to face her friends, her freckled cheeks flushed with excitement. "A week is hardly any time to prepare! We need a strategy if we're going to take back the Golden Ball. The Grimm School has beaten us three years in a row!"

Val seemed about to explain that sprinting to school wouldn't improve Princess School's chances, but Rapunzel had already whirled around again and was dashing up the path. He shrugged at Snow.

"Uh, how is Rose doing?" Val asked hesitantly.

Snow was about to answer when Rapunzel finally slowed down.

"Rose?" Rapunzel echoed, rolling her eyes. "As I've told you the last twenty-six times you've asked, she's fine."

Now it was Val's turn to flush. "I haven't asked about her twenty-six times. I just haven't seen her since the Coronation Ball. So naturally I was wondering how she is. Is she feeling . . . well-rested?"

"Hmmpphhh," Rapunzel said as she turned off the path onto the lane leading to Princess School.

Val was silent for several long moments. Snow

waited to see what would happen. But Val knew Rapunzel well enough to know it was time to change the subject.

"If you really want to win the Maiden Games, you'll need lots of practice and confidence," Val finally said, getting back to Rapunzel's topic of choice.

Once again Rapunzel turned to face him, this time so fast the end of her impossibly long braid nearly whipped him in the face. The braid was actually coiled into a gigantic bun on the back of Rapunzel's head, but the end of it could never be fastened properly and hung down her back past her waist. "Are you saying I lack confidence?" she asked huffily.

Val bowed low to his friend. "Absolutely not," he replied quickly. "I value my life far too much to make such a claim."

"Wise choice," Rapunzel acknowledged, turning back down the lane.

Though she would never say so to Rapunzel, Snow thought Val was right. It *would* take a lot of practice to win the Games. While she knew Rapunzel didn't lack confidence, she was not so sure about herself or the other princesses. Even the oldest girls at Princess School — the Crowns — hadn't seen a victory over the Grimms. And most of the princesses were, well, *princesses* — painfully poised and not very full of sporty

14

gusto. Rapunzel seemed ready for the challenge, but Snow wished the Games weren't even happening.

Lost in thought, Snow did not notice that they were passing by a grove of huge gnarled fruit trees. And then — *thud!* — Val got hit square in the back with something orange, squishy, and rotten.

"Hey!" Val protested, whirling around.

Rapunzel whirled, too. Snow covered her head. But they didn't see anything . . . until they looked up. Leering down at them from high in a leafless persimmon tree hanging with overripe fruit was Hortense Hegbottom, a Grimm School witch.

"Still hungry?" she snickered nastily, swinging her gigantic black boots. "How about another?" She hurled a second moldy persimmon straight into the air. The orange mush-ball rose so high it almost disappeared, then barreled straight down toward Rapunzel so fast it whistled.

Rapunzel's eyes never lost sight of the squishy fruit, and a split second before it careened into the bodice of her gown she ducked. *Splat!* It hit the hard dirt lane and splattered her skirt.

Snow swallowed a scream.

"Thought I might help you practice — being a loser." Hortense's raspy voice reminded Snow of dry leaves. Her broad face and long, pointed nose contorted into a sneer. Tossing another piece of rotting fruit into the air, she casually swung her red-and-black-striped-stockinged legs. "And now I think I'll have a little practice myself . . . with that nest." She waved a fat-knuckled hand at Rapunzel's head and muttered a few words under her breath.

It only took Snow two seconds to figure out what Hortense was up to, but that was two seconds too long. She tried to call out a warning to Rapunzel, but before her long-haired friend could step backward, the branches of the persimmon tree bent dramatically, reaching for her bun. Within moments Rapunzel's reddish-brown coil was half undone. Twine-thick locks stuck out in all directions.

"Hee-hee-hee, and all from a tree," Hortense sang as Val and Snow untangled Rapunzel and pulled her away.

"Ugh, not again," Val complained. "That's two days in a row!"

"At least she didn't open a can of worms on top of *your* head," Rapunzel fumed, shaking a fist at the still-cackling Hortense. "It took me an hour to get this bun in place!"

"Want me to help you fix it?" Snow asked.

Val eyed Rapunzel's hair skeptically.

"No, thanks," Rapunzel said with a frustrated sigh. "I can do it in Looking Glass class."

Snow wished again that the Games were not happening. She felt defeated already. Two witches in one morning were too many! But Rapunzel was raging and even Val seemed energized.

The prince brushed hastily at the orange splotch on his waistcoat. His eyes were bright with excitement. "It's too bad the Charm School doesn't have anyone to compete with," he said. "We could use a little rivalry to shake things up!" He kicked at a pebble in the path. "There's nothing going on at my school but chivalry. I wish I were a girl!"

Chapter Three

A Royal Rally

Though it meant they had to say good-bye to Val, Snow was relieved when the glimmering spires of Princess School finally came into view. It was good to be in the company of friends — and the more friends the better!

"Look, there's Rose and Ella!" she said, taking Rapunzel's arm. Maybe they were talking about something besides the Maiden Games!

Passing under the carved silver archway, Snow and Rapunzel joined their friends. Rose and Ella were looking down at the swans swimming gracefully in the moat. The Coronation Ball tiara still sparkled on Ella's head.

Ella turned to greet them and gasped when she saw the orange splotches on Rapunzel's dress.

"She got you again?" Rose asked. Her blue eyes were wide and her rose-lipped mouth agape at the sight of Rapunzel's hair.

"That ugly little witch has it coming to her," Rapunzel fumed. But even though she scowled, Snow saw another expression in Rapunzel's eyes: exhilaration. She *liked* the competition.

"Hortense's nasty pranks just make me want to win the Maiden Games even more. I'll show her — and all the bratty witches at Grimm!" Rapunzel said with a fiendish grin.

Snow admired her friend's courage and resolve, but as she listened to Rapunzel's words, her breath caught in her throat and she felt numb all over. The images from her nightmares still lingered in her head, along with Lucinta's and Hortense's taunts. Snow was afraid of the Maiden Games — and the Grimms. And for some reason she didn't want to tell her friends how she felt.

"Rapunzel, your hair!" Ella said, reaching up to tuck in a few of the renegade strands.

"Don't bother," Rapunzel replied, blowing a thick auburn curl off her face. "I'll fix it in Looking Glass."

"Good thing it's right after hearthroom," Rose said with a grimace. "No offense, Rapunzel, but it's a *mess*."

"I believe you, and I'm not offended," Rapunzel said flatly. "At least, not by you."

"Weren't you at all frightened?" Snow asked, her dark eyes wide.

"Of course not," Rapunzel replied. "It takes more

than a few rotten persimmons and an enchanted tree to scare me."

"Oh!" Snow said. "I thought it was awful." She saw Ella and Rose exchange smiles, but her face felt frozen as she stared into the moat.

"Is everything all right, Snow?" Ella asked. "You look shaken."

Snow nodded distractedly, her gaze never leaving the smooth, blue-green water below. Everything was not all right. In fact, it was feeling more wrong every minute. But she wasn't sure how to tell her friends. She opened her mouth to speak and closed it again as the two-minute trumpet sounded. Class was about to begin.

The girls climbed the polished marble stairs and the heavy doors to Princess School whooshed open as they approached.

"I'm sure you'll get back at Hortense at the Maiden Games, Rapunzel," Rose said as the girls made their way down the long, tall-ceilinged corridor to hearthroom. Their slippers padded along quietly on the pink-and-white stone floor. All around them golden sunlight glistened off the carved alabaster pillars.

Rapunzel nodded. "Believe me, I intend to," she said with an impish grin.

Behind her, Snow felt an icy chill run up her spine.

Malodora, she thought. Pulling her cape around her shoulders, she followed her friends down the hall.

When the trumpet signaled the end of Hearthroom the first-year Bloomers headed out to the gardens for a special Maiden Games rally. They were followed by the second-year Sashes, the third-year Robes, and finally the fourth-year Crowns.

Snow and her friends made their way past the gleaming statues of famous princesses past and present toward the large Princess School gazebo. Carved stone benches with purple velvet cushions circled an open area with a podium. Celebratory pink banners hung from the rafters, encircling the seating area. At the podium, Headmistress Bathilde stood with her trademark scepter, surrounded by several other teachers.

Snow and her friends found an empty bench near the back and sat down just as Headmistress Bathilde cleared her throat regally.

The gazebo was instantly silent as the princesses waited to hear what Lady Bathilde had to say. The headmistress was not only a beautiful and elegant ruler, she was also a wise and fair guardian of the school.

"Welcome, princesses," she said in her commanding but friendly voice, "to the Princess School Maiden Games rally.

"As those of you who have experienced them before know, the Maiden Games represent many things to our school — sportsprincessship, hard work, team spirit, and honor among them. I want each of you to do your best to be a worthy teammate and competitor at the Games. I'll now turn the proceedings over to our head coach and Self-defense instructor, Madame Lightfoot."

The princesses-in-training clapped delicately as Madame Lightfoot moved to the center of the gazebo. Ella nudged Snow in the side. "We're supposed to clap," she whispered.

Snow smiled weakly and clapped her hands together a few times before the crowd quieted to hear Madame Lightfoot's words.

"This year we are beginning a new tradition of naming four team captains — one from each year — who will help their fellow princesses prepare for the Games and bring all of you together as princesses and competitors. Being team captain is a great honor and also a great responsibility. A panel of teachers, including the headmistress herself, chose this year's captains based on athletic and leadership skills."

Snow looked at the excited faces of the girls seated nearby. Many of them fidgeted in their seats, obviously itching to be named the Bloomer captain. Snow felt nothing. She wished she were anyone in the crowd but herself.

"Per royal etiquette I ask you to please hold your applause until after I have announced all of the team captains.

"The Crown captain will be Astrid Glimmer," Madame Lightfoot read from a scroll. "The Robe captain will be Tiffany Bulugia. The Sash captain will be Antonella Printz. And the Bloomer captain will be . . . Rapunzel Arugula!"

The students burst into hearty applause, momentarily abandoning their proper princess decorum.

Ella let out an excited squeal and squeezed Rapunzel's hand.

"Congratulations!" Snow cried. For the first time all day she felt happy. Rapunzel was a perfect choice!

Rose gave Rapunzel a quick hug. "I knew it would be you!" she said.

"And now for the names of the judges," Madame Lightfoot said. "The Princess School representatives will be Administrator Ballus and Headmistress Bathilde. And from the Grimm School . . . Vermin Twitch and the headmistress, Queen Malodora."

There was a groan from the girls when Vermin Twitch's name was announced.

"He looks like a rat!" a Robe whispered.

"Those beady eyes give me the creeps," added a Sash.

Snow tried to control the shivers that overwhelmed her when the judges were mentioned. But it wasn't Vermin who was upsetting her. She liked rats.

"Practice will begin tomorrow!" Madame Lightfoot declared, ending the rally.

While the rest of the princesses clapped politely, Rapunzel let out a loud whoop and jumped to her feet. Ella and Rose stood to hug and congratulate their friend. In their excitement they didn't notice frozen Snow. Icy fingers gripped the back of Snow's neck and, rooted to her seat, she shook like a bowl of chilled vanilla pudding.

Chapter Four

The Tiara Twist

Perched on her stool in front of a giant mirror in Looking Glass class, Cinderella gazed at the tiara on her head. She had been wearing it for a week and it still took her breath away.

"It's soooo beautiful," said Lisette Iderdown, who was sitting next to her. "It's perfect for you."

Ella blushed. Until recently, she had never thought of herself as beautiful. And to tell the truth, she still didn't. Her blond hair was thick and shiny, and there was nothing really wrong with her face. But she wasn't striking, not like Rose, who was so stunning that more than half the people at school called her "Beauty." But since Ella had been crowned Princess of the Ball a week ago, she'd been getting a lot of attention. She'd gone from being invisible to being . . . well, kind of famous. Every princess in school knew who she was. Older girls — Sashes and even Crowns — stopped her in the halls to ask her opinion about everything from hairdos and gown adornments to how to dance with a boy (she'd done a lot of that at the ball). Even here in Looking Glass class, the teacher, Madame Spiegel, had designed an entire fortnight of classes around tiara hairdos.

Ella loved the attention . . . sort of. It took a lot of work to live up to the crowned princess expectations, and she already had a lot of work to do at home. Her stepmother, Kastrid, and her stepsisters, Hagatha and Prunilla, treated her like a servant. Being crowned at school certainly hadn't changed that. She still had to do all the cooking and cleaning and washing and sewing at home. And now she had to spend extra time on her own hand-me-down gowns, making sure they were clean and perfectly pressed. She was grateful for the honor her new school had bestowed upon her. But sometimes being the center of attention was exhausting. How did Rose do it?

At least Hag and Prune are leaving me alone at school now, Ella thought. They'd managed to make her first two weeks at Princess School simply awful — it was only with the amazing help of her new friends that Ella had made it to the ball at all. But since her steps had made complete fools of themselves in front of *everyone*, including the headmistress, they were now on their best behavior. And Ella had also noticed that Madame Taffeta, her Stitchery teacher, had been watching Hag and Prune closely. Ella was grateful for all of that, but knew better than to expect their silence to last forever.

"It's only a matter of time before they'll be tormenting me again," Ella whispered to her reflection. But then, maybe having things back to normal would be a relief.

"All right, girls," Madame Spiegel said, clapping her hands together and tearing herself away from her own reflected image. "It's time to get to work on our tiara twists." She handed each princess a tiara made of simple silver wire and polished pastel-toned stones. The girls had spent the last week perfecting hairdos that could be worn with crowns: the basic nape-of-the-neck bun, the slightly more advanced French braid tuck, and now the tricky tiara twist.

Once the tiaras had been distributed, Madame Spiegel went back to the giant looking glass at the front of the room. Picking up her comb, she began to divide her blond hair into sections.

"To properly create a tiara twist, you must divide your hair into six equal parts — three per side." She looked over at Rapunzel sympathetically. "Don't worry, Rapunzel," she said. "I'll come help you get your hair under control as soon as I'm finished demonstrating."

"Thank you, Madame Spiegel," Rapunzel said, untangling her massive mess of hair.

One by one, Madame Spiegel took each section of

hair and twisted and coiled it just so. She was so skilled at it that she only needed one hairpin to hold each coil in place.

"After twisting each section several times, you pin it to the side of your head very carefully, maintaining the delicate coil. There should be a curl falling on each side of your face, one over each ear, and one on either side of the nape of your neck. Together they make a complete circle of twists to surround the tiara." Madame Spiegel turned slowly so the princesses could see her hairdo.

"Lovely," said Rose.

Snow nodded blankly.

"My mother says the tiara twist is the perfect princess style," added another Bloomer.

The girls got to work, carefully dividing their long hair into sections. Now and then a frustrated sigh echoed in the tall chamber, but in general the girls seemed excited to try something new. Ella was grateful they didn't think having to learn this tricky style so early was her fault. Normally the tiara twist was part of the Robes' curriculum.

"Do you think we stand a chance at beating the Grimms?" Red, a small friendly girl who always wore a scarlet cape, asked as Ella completed her second twist.

"Definitely," Rapunzel replied as she tried to comb

several tiny twigs out of an auburn lock. "But it's going to take a lot of work — and practice — from all of us."

Ella felt a tingle run up her spine as she remembered the Maiden Games. They sounded so exciting! And she wanted to beat the Grimms as much as she had wanted to see her awful steps get what they deserved for all the trouble they'd caused when they'd hazed the Bloomers earlier in the school year.

Hag and Prune are such witches, they'd be better suited to the Grimm School, Ella thought. She smiled at her reflection as she completed her final twist. *If I'm lucky, they'll get recruited!*

As she began another twist, Ella spotted Snow at a dressing table behind her. Snow was staring wide-eyed at her own reflection and was sitting so still she almost looked like a statue.

Snow hasn't been herself all day, Ella thought as she pinned the twist to the side of her head. *Maybe if I can get her to myself after class I can find out what's bothering her.*

Satisfied with her plan, Ella got back to her tiara twist. She had just pinned the last coil into place when the end-of-class trumpet sounded. It was time for the girls to have their noonday meal in the dining hall. As the princesses spilled into the corridor, Sashes and Bloomers paused to curtsy to Ella. Even Robes and Crowns nodded respectfully.

"There's no need to do that," Ella insisted when Veronique, a popular Robe, momentarily halted her conversation to acknowledge her.

Ella curtsied to Veronique and her cluster of friends before stepping into the dining room. The large chamber was filled with round wooden tables covered with crisp white tablecloths. The gilded silver chairs were ornately carved with roses and ivy to match the pillars found throughout the castle. And the pink-flowered china was as delicate as the most poised of princesses.

Walking with Rose, Ella began to cross the room to get to Snow when a Sash curtsied just inches in front of Ella. Ella tried to return the courtesy, but tripped on the hem of her gown.

"Ugh!" Ella mumbled, steadying herself on a gilded chair just before she fell to the tiled floor. "How do you deal with this, Rose?" Ella asked, straightening up and adjusting her skirt.

"Oh, I suppose you just get used to it," Rose replied. She sounded odd, and didn't look Ella in the eye.

Ella was about to ask Rose if something was wrong when Rapunzel called out from the other end of the room.

"Come on!" she practically shouted. "I've saved us all seats!"

Chapter Five
The Same Path Twice

The trumpets sounded and inside the castle Self-defense class began. Outside, Snow heard the heavy doors close behind her as she raced down the stairs and away from Princess School.

"I'm going to get in terrible trouble for this," she said aloud as she hurried across the bridge. "But I can't bear to stay another minute!"

Snow had been worrying about Malodora and the Maiden Games all day. Ever since the rally she'd wanted to flee the castle. Though she'd almost made it through the day, all the excited talk about the Maiden Games among the other girls finally got to her in Frog ID class. She couldn't even smile when a little green guy had croaked a froggy song to her. As soon as class was over she'd made a dash for the door.

Snow knew she owed it to her school and her friends to do her best at the competitions. Rapunzel was one of the captains! But her stepmother was one of the judges — and Snow just couldn't face her! She was torn between fear and friends. What was she going to do? Perhaps she would be able to sort out her thoughts in her cozy cottage.

I'm not going anywhere near Grimm, Snow thought with a shudder as she followed the lane that led away from the smoke-stained castle. It was the long way home. *The very last thing I need is another encounter with awful Lucinta Pintch!*

As Snow walked down the path, she pictured Lucinta's face. Her beady black eyes reminded Snow of a weasel she once caught stealing eggs from a robin's nest.

"Nasty witchy weasel!" Snow said aloud, startling herself. It wasn't like her to say anything mean, even about a witch.

Snow tried to put the entire terrible day out of her mind as she picked her way along the shadowy path. She puckered her lips and tried to whistle the cereal song. She couldn't remember it. It was lost in her head. And suddenly Snow felt lost in the woods. She looked around for familiar landmarks. Though she knew she had chosen the safer route, an uneasy yet familiar feeling came over her . . . the feeling that someone was watching her.

Above her the sky was light, with a few clouds scattered here and there. But the forest was dark and the branches seemed to reach down to her.

Her heart thudded in her chest and Snow picked up her pace, moving more quickly through the forest. The path led deeper and deeper into darkness, and rocks and gnarled tree roots made the route treacherous. Still, Snow moved faster and faster until she finally broke into a run. Branches above and beneath her creaked and snapped, and the howls of forest animals echoed in the distance. Snow was dismayed to realize that even this normally comforting sound was now terrifying to her.

An icy finger snaked its way up her spine, and Snow turned, certain that someone was behind her. But the darkened path was empty. Turning back, Snow raced ahead, dark shadows swirling around her. As branches and leaves swiped at her face, she suddenly realized she was not lost. She had taken this path before . . . when she fled her father's castle.

With tears streaming down her pale face, Snow White stumbled out of the dense forest and fuzzily saw the dwarf cottage in a clearing before her. Sobbing, she ran toward it, burst through the door, and flew up the stairs. Her tiny alcove room was a welcome sight, but she was too distraught to do anything but cross to the wooden bed the dwarves carved for her when she'd moved in. Exhausted, threw herself across the sweet-smelling straw-filled mattress and fell fast asleep.

No sooner had her eyes closed than Snow White began to dream. There was the ocean, blue-green with lapping waves. Then a ship appeared and, with it, a howling wind. Rain poured from the sky, and waves began to pound the sides of the seemingly tiny boat. Then suddenly, Snow's father appeared on deck! He was calling Snow's name, Snow was sure, but the wind and rain were carrying the cries away as quickly as he uttered them. The tattered sails blew wildly in the wind. With a final desperate cry, Snow's father fell to his knees. . . .

Snow sobbed and turned in her sleep and the scene before her eyes shifted dramatically. Suddenly Snow was back at her father's castle — a little girl playing happily in the orchards. Apple blossoms rained down on her rosy cheeks, dusting her eyelids. Above her, she saw her father's face as he playfully shook the branches of the apple tree. But then the shimmering castle beyond the blooming trees transformed into a dark, soot-stained fortress.

Snow was instantly inside, following her stepmother up a darkened staircase to her attic workshop. Dim torches cast more shadow than light and the air was dank and stale.

Malodora's eyes shimmered with evil as she threw

open a door to another, smaller chamber. Heaped on the floor were dead rodents of all shapes and sizes — moles, squirrels, shrews, mice, and rats.

"Noooo!" Snow screamed, turning her eyes away from the poor dead creatures. Whirling on her heel, she raced down the stairs and out of the castle back to the orchards . . . the only place in the castle where she could still feel her father's presence, the place they walked together on many an afternoon, smelling the blossoms and picking the luscious fruit. And then Snow felt her father's strong, comforting arms around her waist as he lifted her high to pick a ripe and perfect apple. . . .

With a jolt, Snow sat up in bed. Tears streamed down her face. Looking around her small room, she felt lonely and relieved all at once. Her father was gone, but so was Malodora. Snow was in her cozy woodland cottage and safe . . . at least for the moment.

Chapter Six
Admiration and Envy

It seemed like an eternity before the final trumpet sounded, announcing the end of the school day. Rose didn't think she'd ever watched the hourglass on Madame Taffeta's desk so closely. At times it felt like the sand was running backward!

Rose was in such a hurry to find out what was going on with Snow that she rushed out of class and onto the steps at the entrance of the school without stopping to put her texts and scrolls in her trunk. It was a mistake. Now, as she stood alone, her books weighed heavily in her arms. And she had to wait for Ella and Rapunzel to catch up — they were probably stuck in the mobbed hallway putting *their* stuff away so they could travel light.

Sinking down to sit on the polished stone landing, Rose felt anxious. Her chest was tight. It felt like there was something caught inside it — a sigh maybe, or a sob. She was really worried about Snow. But there was something else wrong, too. Something she couldn't quite name.

With a rustle of skirts and the patter of slippers on stone, the landing at the top of the stairs was flooded with princesses. Rose could hear the excitement in their voices as they chatted about the Maiden Games, but at the moment she did not share it.

As a group of especially talkative girls began to flow past her, Rose realized they were all focused on someone in the middle of the swarm. Something shiny sparkled in the center of the girls. Rose recognized the glint. It was Ella's tiara.

As she watched Ella soak up attention from the other girls, the tightness in Rose's chest threatened to split her wide open.

What is wrong with me? Rose wondered, hugging her texts tightly. Only last week this same swarm of girls was buzzing around Rose. The attention had been annoying — exhausting even. But in some ways, Rose had to admit, it had been nice to be admired — or at least noticed.

Rose brushed her skirts and forced a smile in Ella's direction. Ella was her friend. Rose should be happy for her. If anyone deserved attention it was Ella. Didn't she have to put up with her horrible stepfamily? Hadn't she spent enough of her life being harassed? She could use a little admiration!

A hundred thoughts buzzing in her head, Rose leaned back on one hand.

"Ouch!"

Intent on what Ella was saying (something about the dress she'd made for Hagatha), a fawning princess stepped right on Rose's fingers. "Oh, sorry, Rose!" she said quickly. But an instant later she had turned back so as not to miss another of Ella's words.

Rose fumed, sucking on her crushed finger. Last week that same girl had been calling her "Beauty"! It was such a silly nickname; Rose always thought she hated it. But at the moment she actually missed it. A lot.

Rose got to her feet. "Don't you feel a little silly wearing that tiara *every* day?" she asked, speaking a little more loudly than she'd meant to.

Ella's face turned bright pink as the crowd around her fell silent. She touched the jeweled crown self-consciously. "It's traditional," she replied, looking hurt and a little confused. "The Princess of the Ball wears it until the closing ceremony of the Maiden Games. "I just . . ." she trailed off, too surprised and confused to go on. For a moment, Ella and Rose stared at each other in silence. Then Rose looked away.

At last Rapunzel burst out of the Princess School

doors and waved frantically at her friends. Rose met her on the edge of the top step, and as they waited for Ella to break free of her fans Rapunzel spoke to the rest of the students on the stairs.

"Don't forget to come to Maiden Games practice tomorrow morning! We'll start the warm-up at the cock's first crow!" Rapunzel said loudly.

Several of the girls groaned. It was barely light at first crow! But Rapunzel was unmoved. "We want to win the Golden Ball, don't we?" she asked with her arms wide.

"Yes!" the girls chorused as they headed down the stairs.

"Okay, then." Rapunzel planted her fists on her hips and gave a little nod. Then in a quieter voice Rapunzel spoke to Rose and Ella. "Now, let's go find Snow."

The farther they got from Princess School the better Rose felt. It was good to be with her friends. When she wasn't surrounded by adoring girls, Rose could see that Ella was still just Ella. Besides, it felt great to finally be on their way to Snow's house after worrying all through Self-defense.

"I don't know what would make Snow take off like that." Ella shook her head.

"I know she's nervous about the games," Rose said.

"But it's not like Snow to worry," Rapunzel put in. "She's *always* cheery."

Rose had to agree. Something was seriously wrong.

Moving quickly, Rose followed Rapunzel and Ella down a path she'd never been on before. Rapunzel knew all of the trails in the woods and insisted this was the fastest one. But it was dark and narrow and the trees grew close on either side, meeting overhead and almost completely blocking out the autumn sun. Rose usually traveled by carriage with about a dozen guards. It was a little creepy slogging through the forest this way. But seeing Rapunzel's massive reddish bun and Ella's shining locks and sparkling crown bobbing ahead of her was enough reassurance to keep her going.

"Look!" Rapunzel called as they approached a clearing. "It's Grimm!" Indeed, the back side of the towering black castle loomed over them.

Rose had never seen the Grimm School from this angle before. Her heartbeat quickened a little as she stepped off the path and peered past the ornate gingerbread fence surrounding the school. The Grimm castle was oily black with brackish moss growing on the square stone walls. Smoke belched out of smokestacks and even from the windows of some of the towers. Rose wasn't sure whether it was coming from wood fires, the kitchens, or spells gone wrong. Besides the sickly mosses on the castle stones, there wasn't a single patch of green on the Grimm School grounds. All of the grass was dry and brown — perhaps killed by the acrid smoke. And the only plant that dared to approach the tall, narrow building was a bloodred creeping ivy vine that circled one of the towers like a tightening rope.

Rose shivered.

"There's nothing we can't handle here," Rapunzel said encouragingly, not altering her course to avoid walking right past the gingerbread gate. "Besides, the witches have all gone home."

Rose was starting to relax a little when she heard a *whoosh* overhead. Ella grabbed her elbow and the girls looked up in time to catch a flash of black-and-red stocking as a nasty-looking witch swooped by on a ratty broom. Rose stole a look at Rapunzel. From the way she was glaring, Rose knew the girl had to be Hortense Hegbottom, the same witch who had messed with Rapunzel that morning, and the morning before. But Rapunzel didn't look scared, just mad.

"Three little princesses, pretty as can be . . ." The wide-faced witch cackled, circling over Rose and her friends, obviously enjoying herself. Then with eyes filled with scorn, Hortense raised a red-knuckled finger and pointed at the gate. The pretty gingerbread swung open so quickly it slammed into Rapunzel and knocked her over. Rapunzel landed on the damp dirt with a thud.

"One got wholloped and landed on her knees!" Hortense finished her rhyme and swooped lower to laugh in Rapunzel's face before she could pull herself back to her feet. "A perfect position for you," Hortense sneered. "I suggest you get used to it. You'll be begging for mercy at the Maiden Games."

Then Hortense turned to study Ella and Rose more carefully. Her broom hummed in one place — a hovering seat — and she casually swung her sturdy legs back and forth just inches above the ground. Hortense smiled wider, revealing large yellowed teeth.

"These must be your teammates," she cackled. "Aren't they lovely!" Then the nasty witch began to laugh so hard she nearly fell off her broomstick.

One look at Rapunzel and Rose knew they had to get her out of there — fast — or Rapunzel was going to make trouble. She pushed past Hortense and helped Rapunzel to her feet, keeping a tight grip on her arm to prevent her friend from launching herself at Hortense.

"Let's go," Ella said softly, taking Rapunzel's other arm and backing away. "We'll get our chance to retaliate at the Games."

Luckily Rapunzel was too angry to speak. She was casting daggers with her eyes, but they weren't penetrating Hortense's armor. With a heavy thunk, Hortense flipped off her broom and lay on the dirt, howling and pounding it with her fist.

The sound of her laughter followed them down the trail, and only after it had disappeared completely did Rapunzel find her tongue.

"Who does that witch think she is?" she asked, practically shouting. "And what does she mean saying we're 'lovely'? Lovely's got nothing to do with it!"

Rose couldn't have agreed more, but she knew better than to feed Rapunzel's fire. "Don't worry, captain. She'll see how lovely we are when we're holding the Golden Ball."

Rapunzel snorted, but seemed to calm down a little. By the time they made it to Snow's cottage she was almost her normal self.

"This must be it," Ella said, gazing at the small stone cottage in a grassy clearing. It was adorable and neat as a pin. The grass had been trimmed all around the house, and a large pile of carefully stacked firewood stood under a small lean-to along with a sturdy wheelbarrow and a collection of garden tools. Wildflowers and shrubs of all kinds grew in the garden in front of the house, and a few potted plants bloomed beautifully on the front porch.

Ella hurried ahead and knocked on the small door, which was painted bright red.

"Snow!" Rose called up to the eight round windows on the second floor. Each window had its own small window box bursting with flowers, and beneath the sod roof the rafters of the house were carved into the shapes of different animals.

"Snow!" Rapunzel echoed Rose's call, but didn't bother to knock. She opened the front door and strode inside, Ella and Rose at her heels.

At the end of a long but rather short dining table Snow sat, slumped over a giant bowl filled with applesauce. Empty jars were strewn everywhere, along with several sticky spoons. Snow looked up and a lump of sauce slowly slid down her face to drip off the end of her quivering chin. The poor girl's dark eyes were rimmed with tears and her usually lovely pale skin was red and covered in splotches.

Chapter Seven
An Apple a Day

Nothing was working. Usually when Snow was blue, a little bowl of applesauce was all she needed to sweeten her mood. She'd eaten seven and she was still miserable. Sniffing, Snow spooned up another bite. She couldn't let the dwarves see her like this — she just had to cheer up! Letting one last tear drip into her bowl, she closed her eyes and tried to picture Hap's face. Nobody could resist that cheerful dwarf's smile.

Suddenly the door to the cottage opened with a *bang*. Snow felt panic surge within her.

There in the doorway stood Snow's friends — Rapunzel, Ella, and Rose. Worry showed on their faces.

"Oh, Snow!" Ella rushed forward and threw her arms around the sauce-covered girl.

Seeing her friends should have made Snow feel better, but it only made her feel worse. A fresh flood of tears poured onto Ella's shoulder.

"What is it?" Rapunzel asked.

"Did something happen to the dwarves?" Rose wanted to know.

"Oh gosh, no." Snow sniffed. "Well, gee, I hope not." Now she had something new to worry about. But all she really wanted was to keep other people from worrying about her. Snow hiccuped.

"You have to tell us what's the matter," Rapunzel said gently, easing the large applesauce spoon out of her hand. "We can help, I know it."

"It's nothing, really." Snow watched Rose carry an empty applesauce jar to the sink along with her bowl. "I just . . . well . . ." She gazed at the floor. "I just can't face the Maiden Games. I can't go."

"Oooh." Rapunzel sounded relieved. "You don't have to worry about the Games! You'll be fine. Of course we all need to practice. But by game day —"

"No." Snow shook her head. That wasn't it. She knew she wasn't exactly the fiercest competitor — it was always so much more fun to see someone else win — but she wasn't afraid to try. She was afraid of something much scarier.

Snow hiccuped and felt Ella's arm across her shoulders. She hadn't realized she was trembling.

"You can tell us," Ella coaxed.

"We're your friends." Rose nodded, wiping a tear

from Snow's cheek with her sleeve. "You can always tell us anything."

With another hiccup Snow finally managed to say what was really bothering her. "It's my stepmother, Malodora. She's been watching me — I can feel it. And I've been having nightmares."

Rapunzel and Ella exchanged looks.

"It's that mirror," Snow went on between hiccups. "She sees me in it. It turns her against me!" Snow hadn't wanted to burden her friends with all this, but it felt good to finally tell somebody what was bothering her.

"I just don't understand. She is so mean to me. I think she's . . . jealous!" Snow finally put it into words. "She didn't understand that people were nice to me because I was nice to them." Snow slumped in her seat with a final hiccup, exhausted.

Her friends looked at her with big eyes, waiting to hear more.

"So I ran away," Snow said, wiping the applesauce off her chin. "I knew Malodora was going to put a spell on me like she did my father. So I ran, and ended up here — with my dwarves." Snow took a deep breath and let the sight of the peaceful cottage kitchen comfort her. She felt her breathing get closer to normal and the warmth of her friends' hands on hers. "I guess

I've been pretty safe here." She sighed. "I felt her watching me for a while, but then it stopped. Maybe if I'm not in Malodora's way, she doesn't hate me so much. But lately, ever since they announced the Games, she's been looking in that mirror again. She's been watching me. And I've been having nightmares." Snow shuddered. "Horrible nightmares!"

"Do you think Malodora sends them?" Ella asked. "My stepmother, Kastrid, is awful, but at least she doesn't have magical powers."

"Do you think she can see us now?" Rapunzel narrowed her eyes and glared around the room.

"When she's looking I can feel it," Snow explained. "It feels like a chill — like someone is sneaking up behind me. And sometimes I feel icy fingers on my neck."

Rose looked like she might cry. "How awful!"

"Hic!" Snow's hiccups returned. She picked up a nearly empty jar of applesauce from the table and clinked a stray spoon around the bottom, looking for a last bite. "That's why I can't go to the Games. She's already watching me. If I get in her way, she'll do something awful, I just know it!

"Hic. She might use a spell. Hic. She might never let my father come home. Hic. Or she might hurt the dwarves. Hic. Hic. Hic. Besides, I just freeze in front of her. If she's a judge at the Games, I won't be any help to anyone."

"You are always a help, Snow, to all of us." Rapunzel pried the applesauce jar out of Snow's porcelain hands.

Rose and Ella nodded as they quickly cleared away the remaining jars and spoons.

"We can get through this," Rose said.

"Together!" Ella added, starting to work the pump for the sink. "We can get through anything together."

Rose took over the pump, and Ella sat down on the low bench next to Snow. "Look how we got around *my* evil stepmother." Ella smiled.

"We won't let anything happen to you," Rapunzel said. "I promise." She shook out a flour sack towel with a snap. "And I promise you something else, too. We are going to beat Malodora and her Grimm girls. For Princess School, and for you!"

Feeling better than she had in days, Snow got to her feet and hugged her friends. Maybe she *could* face her stepmother if she didn't have to do it alone — if she had Rose, Ella, and Rapunzel beside her.

While Snow helped Rose and Ella finish washing and drying the applesauce dishes, Rapunzel got comfortable by the hearth scratching out game plans on the slate with a charred stick.

In the cozy firelight, Snow didn't notice that it was getting dark outside. And over the happy chatter of her friends, she didn't hear the low humming of the dwarves' voices as they made their way home.

"Ho, ho!" exclaimed Mort as he threw open the cottage door. "Where's our Snow?" he called. But he stopped short when he saw the four girls in the kitchen. Then his already-cheerful face broke into a wide grin.

Hap clapped his hands together and danced around excitedly, catching Wheezer's hands and pulling him into the jig. "Company! We have company!" he cried.

"More mouths means more dishes!" Gruff groused.

Peeking over Gruff's shoulder, Meek waved a single stubby finger at Snow and her three friends before disappearing again behind Gruff's huge backpack.

Taking charge like he usually did, Mort gently elbowed Hap and Wheezer out of the way and stepped up to Ella.

"Introductions!" he declared out of the corner of his mouth. While Mort took Ella's hand and bowed, Hap and Wheezer fell in line behind him, followed by a reluctant Gruff and, finally, Meek.

"Oh." Ella giggled when Mort kissed her hand. "I'm not really royalty. Not yet, anyway."

Mort looked at the tiara on Ella's head and raised his eyebrows.

"This is Ella," Snow jumped in.

"Oh, yes, the belle of the ball." Mort nodded. "And this beauty must be Briar Rose." Mort kissed Rose's hand next before moving on to Rapunzel. "And you are the maiden in the tower, I presume?"

"Rapunzel," she said, introducing herself. "We've heard all about you, too."

"Ah . . . ah . . . ah'm Wheezer," Wheezer managed to put in before burying his face in a handkerchief.

"And this is Gruff and Hap and, behind that chair is Meek," Mort added.

"That's only five," Rose counted. "Aren't there seven of you?"

Crash! A sturdy wooden wheelbarrow suddenly plowed into the room and rolled onto its side, spilling a sixth dwarf onto the floor, but not waking him.

"Nod," Rose said knowingly.

"And you must be Dim." Ella put out her hand to the dwarf driving the wheelbarrow. The little man looked at it blankly for a moment and then handed her his backpack.

The four girls burst out laughing, and Snow felt warm all over. She hadn't expected to be introducing her friends to the dwarves today. Now, with the cottage filled with so many of her favorite people, thoughts of her stepmother felt far away. And everyone seemed to be enjoying one another.

Rose helped Nod find a comfortable chair to doze in while Rapunzel loaded Dim into the wheelbarrow and pushed it back out of the kitchen. Mort and Ella looked like they were deep in conversation. Hap was still dancing with a sneezing Wheezer, and Gruff's wrinkled forehead looked a little smoother than usual as he took a seat at the table, ready for his evening meal.

"Oh." Snow put her hand to her mouth. She had forgotten all about supper.

"Don't you worry about supper," Mort said, patting Snow on the shoulder. "You haven't been yourself lately, my dear, and time with friends is just what you need. Besides," he added, placing a chubby hand on his round belly and giving Ella a sideways look, "you might even say we're a little *too* well fed. We'll get our own supper."

"Hmph." The furrow in Gruff's brow returned as he slid back off the bench. "And do our own dishes, too, I suppose," he muttered. But the rest of the dwarves seemed thrilled to dip into the larder and come up with something to eat.

"Stay for supper!" Hap called to the girls as he scooped flour into a big wooden bowl.

"Ah-chood." Wheezer nodded, seconding the motion and spraying flour all over Nod.

"Please?" Meek said faintly from under the bench where he'd been drumming out a rhythm with a pair of forks.

"I wish I could," Rapunzel said. "I have to get back

to my tower before Madame Gothel suspects something."

"And I have chores," Ella moaned.

Snow thought she saw Ella's eyes following Hap as he gleefully tossed two apples, a potato, and a half a loaf of bread into the pot of water hanging over the fire.

Rose glanced at the setting sun and bit her lip. "It's getting late. My parents will be worried sick," she said. "I told them we might have practice for the Games, but they'll be expecting me now. And they might send out a search party if I don't show up soon."

"Yes, yes." Mort nodded like a teeny grandfather. "Mustn't worry the parents." Mort walked the girls to the door, bowing and kissing their hands again. The rest of the dwarves had erupted into a raucous song about hasty, tasty vittles. They yelled good-byes, blowing kisses between verses.

Snow couldn't keep a smile off her face as she stood beside her funny family and watched her good friends disappear down the path. Maybe everything would be all right after all.

Chapter Eight
A Less-Than-Perfect Practice

The sky was pink with morning sun as Ella trotted onto the large field where the princesses were holding their practices. A quartet of pavilions — two for each school — had already been set up on the field to house equipment and the official rule scrolls of the Games. Though the Grimms practiced on the same field, they were scheduled to use it at different times.

Ella had gotten up and started her chores before the rooster had even rolled out of his nest that morning, but she was still late. The field was already bustling with princesses crowded around scribes scribbling names on sign-up scrolls. Ella gave a quick wave to Rose and a pale, but smiling, Snow, and hurried over to Rapunzel, who was directing traffic. She hoped she wasn't too late to put her name on the list for something good.

"Once you have signed up, please report to your

captains for warm-ups!" Rapunzel barked. "We have to get in some playtime before hearthroom." She turned to Ella. "So, what are you going out for? Unicornshoes? Spinning Straw into Gold? Maze to Grandmother's?"

Ella wasn't sure what she wanted to do.

"Spinning is out for you, Rose," Snow said gravely. Her skin was still a little splotchy around her mouth, but she looked a lot better than yesterday. The others agreed Rose should stay away from sharp objects — especially spindles. Ever since the pinprick that brought on Rose's sleepy episode before the Coronation Ball, her friends were nearly as protective of her as her parents.

Ella knew she didn't want to do Spinning, either — it was too much like the drudgery she had to do at home. The Delicate Touch competition might be okay, or the Gingerbread Man Chase. Surely she could catch a cookie. But could she catch it before a Grimm girl? Ella wanted to be sure she could do more than just play. She wanted to win.

Ella was sure that her classmates had the talent. And she was sure they could win without the terrible cheating tactics of the Grimm girls or the help of Hagatha and Prunilla, who had gotten a decree from home excusing them from participation.

Good riddance, Ella thought. *The Princess School team is better off without them.*

Lost in thought, Ella almost fell over when Rapunzel nudged her toward a page holding a large feathered quill. "You and Rose should do the Lace Race," she said. "We need a strong team."

The Lace Race! That will be perfect, Ella thought. She imagined running beside Rose with their inside legs tightly bound together with several pieces of delicate lace. *We'll be a great team. All we have to do is work together*.

"Oh, I wish I was on Ella's team," a nearby princess said quietly to her friend. Ella waited for the admiring girls to step aside politely so she could sign up.

She smiled at Rose as she gave her name to the scribe. But Rose didn't smile back.

She must be nervous about the Games, Ella told herself. She couldn't blame her. There was more than just the trophy at stake now. They needed to win for Snow. While Ella truly believed they could win the Games, she had no idea how it was going to happen.

The competition was going to be tough. The princesses would have to deal with elbowing and tripping and cheating, but Ella could only imagine what the Grimm girls would have to face from their headmistress if they lost. Malodora looked like she would revel in doling out punishments, and after what Snow had told them last night . . . Ella shuddered. Even if they didn't win, Ella was grateful she would be playing on the Princess School team.

"Oh, Ella, are you going out for Lace Race, too?"

An elegant Sash sidled up to Ella, looking admiringly at her tiara.

Wow. Ella smiled back at the other girls, unsure what to say. She had never had so many people trying to be her friend! Luckily Rapunzel intervened.

"We only need one more team for Lace Race. But I'm looking for a few princesses who are good at guessing. Who wants to play Guess the Little Man's Name?"

"I can do that," the Sash replied.

"And we need some hearty souls to join me on the team for Full Contact Maypole." Rapunzel pointed the way to another scribe, and seven well-postured princesses followed her orders. Enough for a team.

"Maypole is one of the toughest events of the Maiden Games." Rapunzel shook her head and talked in low tones to Rose, Ella, and Snow. "It almost always goes to the Grimm side. But this year *I'll* be playing." Rapunzel winked and scurried off to make sure her team got signed up properly.

"What are you going out for, Snow?" Ella asked, trying to distract her friend. The pale girl hadn't hummed a note yet that morning. Though she put on a brave face, Ella knew she was still nervous.

"I guess I'm doing Ball Fetch. Rapunzel says all I have to do is ask a frog to retrieve a ball from the bottom of a spring. The Grimm witches use threats. But Rapunzel says I have a way with animals."

"You do." Ella nodded. Ball Fetch was the perfect game for Snow!

"Animals love you," Rose added.

"Well, I love them, you know." Snow smiled for the first time all morning, then pulled her cloak tighter around her neck.

In the center of the field, Astrid Glimmer, the Crown captain, put a large horn to her lips and produced a most undignified sound. All the girls scattered on the field looked up as she began an announcement. "My royal teammates. We have a full roster for each of the events." Several girls applauded politely. "Let the practice commence!"

Each captain held up a large banner on a pole, indicating which event she would direct. The princesses walked in orderly fashion to their various groups. Ella and Rose's event wasn't up yet, so they stood on the sidelines watching the other girls.

She was no expert, but Ella could tell things were off to a rocky start.

The Unicornshoe throwers were awful. The first girl to try a toss couldn't get the U-shaped shoe even close to the spiraled horn sticking out of the ground. The second girl spun around for speed and ended up throwing the shoe behind her, whacking one of the Maypole players in the shin. As the Maypole player limped off the field with the back of her hand held to her forehead, trying not to swoon, the thrower fell to her knees and begged forgiveness.

On other parts of the field, things were even worse.

"I'm exhausted," one of the Maze runners complained. She'd barely made it halfway to Grandmother's House when she fell to the ground in a heap and yelped as she landed on a tiny toadstool.

"I'm hungry," Gretel cried, watching the Gingerbread Man run into the woods.

"Princesses, please!" Rapunzel yelled so loudly that every girl on the field stopped and looked at her.

If Ella didn't know better, she would have been frightened of her friend. Rapunzel stood with her hands on her hips. Her coiled hair made her appear taller than most of the older girls. And the look on her face said quite clearly, "Don't mess with me."

"Heed my words. We must all do our royal best. While we will always demonstrate good conduct and sportsprincessship, we will never get anywhere if we give up before we begin. We need practice! Practice is the key to winning. I want to see you all working harder and doing your best. Yes, your gloves will get dirty and your dresses will get stained. But we must endure if we want to win!"

Everyone stared at Rapunzel. Ella knew her friend

had the best of intentions, but this drilling wasn't doing any good. The princesses looked like cornered kittens. No one made a sound.

Suddenly the silence was broken by a loud buzzing and crackling. Ella looked up and gasped. In the sky above the field, two smoky messages slowly appeared behind a pair of Grimm witches riding broomback: BEAT THE BLOOMERS! DOWN WITH CROWNS!

Chapter Nine

Smoke Choke

Thick green smoke drifted down and settled over the stunned princesses on the field. Rapunzel coughed. Ugh! As if the sky taunts weren't bad enough, the smoke they were written in smelled *horrible* — a cross between rotten eggs and kitchen slop.

The satin sleeve covering Rapunzel's nose didn't keep her eyes from watering. On the sidelines Snow, Ella, and Rose breathed into their capes. Through her tears Rapunzel saw the two witches who had left the messages howling on their broomsticks.

"You think you're crying now — just wait until Game day!" one of them spat. As the smoke cleared, the witches flew away, growing smaller and smaller in the distance until they looked like tiny, irritating gnats.

Rapunzel uncovered her face and looked around the field. Everywhere novice princesses were coughing into lacy handkerchiefs and dabbing their eyes. It was clear that practice was over even before the ten-minute trumpet sounded, alerting them school would soon begin. The girls rushed off the field, relieved.

"After school we'll pick up where we left off," Rapunzel called. "Meet right here!"

Watching her classmates flee, Rapunzel suddenly had an awful thought. *What if it's the practice they're trying to get away from and not just the stench?*

Lost in thought and oblivious to the smell, Rapunzel walked slowly behind the others. She had to find a way to get her classmates to enjoy practice, to try harder, to want to win as much as she did. Reaching inside her pocket she felt the small, smooth hand mirror she always kept with her so she could communicate with Val over at the Charm School for Boys. That was it! She would flash Val a message to meet her in the stables at lunch. He would have some good ideas for inspiring the princesses. Feeling decidedly better, Rapunzel skipped the rest of the way up the steps.

Whatever was in the nasty green smoke seemed to have colored the mood at Princess School. Unlike yesterday, the girls were quiet. They were not passing small scrolls or whispering excitedly about the Games. In fact, nobody was talking about the Games at all — it was as if they thought that if the competition wasn't mentioned, it might just disappear. Not even Snow and Ella were talking. Rose seemed positively wilted.

Maybe the smoke was a spell, Rapunzel thought. If it was, it was a good one. Princess School didn't stand a chance at the Maiden Games without any enthusiasm. The closer lunch got, the more anxious Rapunzel was to talk to Val.

It felt like a lifetime before the trumpeters finally sounded the horns. When they did, Rapunzel was off like a fox fleeing a hunting party. She raced down the hall, slipping on the polished stones and sliding out the front door and down the steps. She arrived at the stables out of breath.

Since it was lunchtime, she and Val would have the stables to themselves.

"I'm so . . . glad . . . you're here," Rapunzel panted at Val.

He was sitting on a bale of hay in their regular stall. When he saw Rapunzel, his mouth spread into a grin. "I told you I would be! Have I ever let you down?"

"Not yet." Rapunzel slumped down next to the prince.

"Tell me everything," Val said. "We smelled something over at Charm. Everyone's saying it's the Grimms' choke smoke!"

"Yep." Rapunzel finally caught her breath. "They wrote us a few messages this morning."

"On broomsticks?" Val's eyes were wide.

Rapunzel nodded and told him all about the terrorizing witches. Val's eyes got bigger and bigger. He was enjoying the story so much Rapunzel couldn't help laying it on a little thick. "We could barely see to get off the field," she finished, shaking her head. Then she remembered the real trouble — the pouting princesses.

"But that's not the worst of it," she said, getting serious. "Even before the Grimms came around, the practice was terrible! No matter how much I yelled, nobody wanted to work harder."

"So you have your work cut out for you." Val said.

"I'm pretty sure we can take the Delicate Touch competition," Rapunzel said. "Princesses have it over witches in that category every time, if you ask me."

Val nodded as Rapunzel went on. "Grimms can't seem to touch that lace tapestry softly no matter what tricks they try. They tear the ancient fabric practically every time. Snow's going to do the Ball Fetch, so that's in the bag. And even though we haven't practiced it yet, Lace Race should be all sewn up." Rapunzel was beginning to ramble, but Val was listening intently.

"We don't have anyone to compete in the Apple Bob. We didn't even put it on the roster. There is just no convincing a princess to willingly get her head wet.

And we might as well just give Grimm the Guess the Little Man's Name and the Gingerbread Man Chase. Oh! If you could have seen the mess around the Maypole!"

Talking even faster, Rapunzel described the tangle of streamers and the toppled girls that were the result of Full Contact Maypole practice. "We were supposed to just walk through it — to get the feel of it. All we need is to get one member of our team to circle the pole ten times without losing hold of a ribbon attached to the top. During the actual Games, another team will be trying to wind their ribbons in the other direction — and keep us from winding ours. But we can't even get it right when we're all alone. I was yelling so loud I'm surprised you didn't hear me." Rapunzel rolled her eyes. "And I practically lost my voice trying to get a few girls to pick up the pace during the Maze to Grandmother's House run-through.

"Honestly, if I don't get this team going, we are going to stink worse than the choke smoke!"

When Rapunzel finally finished ranting, the stable fell silent except for the occasional horse blowing breath or pawing the straw-covered floor. Val squinted a little and tilted his chin toward the peak of the vaulted ceiling. It was a look Rapunzel recognized — he was thinking *hard*.

"So?" Rapunzel said impatiently.

"I think you need to tell them they're doing great," Val said slowly.

"But they're not!" Rapunzel cried, exasperated. Hadn't Val listened to a single word she'd said?

"Listen to me," Val said calmly. "They need encouragement. Tell them they are fantastic — better than you imagined. Tell them the Golden Ball is as good as yours."

"I would be lying." Rapunzel scowled. Obviously Val was not going to help her out on this one.

"Rapunzel," Val said, putting a hand on her shoulder, "you know you are my best friend. But once in a while you are too tough, even on me. Imagine how the princesses feel. They are used to a certain amount of pampering. You can't force them to get better. You have to make them believe they can. And you have to make them want to do it . . . for Princess School and for you."

Rapunzel wasn't sure what to say. She hated when Val used his kingly speech voice on her. But she couldn't really argue with what he'd said. For a long moment she looked up at the rays of sunlight slanting through the rafters and watched the dust motes settle. "I better get back," she said at last, heading out of the stall.

"Just think about it," Val called after her. "Okay?"

"Okay," Rapunzel replied, pushing open the stable door.

"Promise?" Val said, coming after her.

Rapunzel sighed. Val was a good match for her, sometimes too good. "Promise!" she yelled, breaking into a run. She was already thinking about it, and by the time the doors to Princess School whooshed open to greet her, she knew what she would do.

Chapter Ten
On the Right Path

When the trumpeters sounded the end of the day, the lump in Snow's stomach suddenly felt bigger. She gathered her texts and scrolls together and made her way through the crowded corridors to her velvet-lined trunk to drop off her things and get her practice pantaloons. Then she headed into the princess powder room to change.

Inside, it was crowded. The lace-curtained changing compartments were all occupied, and the girls who already had on their pantaloons and short gowns were bustling in front of the dressing table mirrors, pinning their hair up. The girls moved slowly. Nobody seemed eager to get onto the practice field.

"I wish we didn't have another practice," said Genevieve, the Goose Girl, as she secured a final strand of hair. "My eyes have just stopped watering from that horrible smoke. My handkerchief is filthy!"

"Ready to go, Snow?" said a voice beside her. It was Rose, already in pantaloons and practice-appropriate hair. Ella appeared a moment later from behind a compartment curtain.

"I still have to change," Snow said, slipping into the compartment Ella had just come out of. As she pulled her high-collared gown off over her head, she took a deep breath.

Everything is going to be fine, she told herself. But her words didn't help. She was grateful to her friends for trying to help her get through this. But her heart was still filled with dread.

Ella peeked behind the curtain. Her hair was already in a neat bun, and her tiara sparkled beautifully. "Almost done?" she asked. "We don't want to be late!"

"Our captain says it's our job to set a good example," Rose said with a mock-serious expression.

"Indeed." Ella sighed.

Flanked by her friends, Snow followed the other princesses out onto the practice field. Snow spied Rapunzel on the other end of the playing field, in a huddle with the other coaches.

"Let's gather over here!" Astrid Glimmer called, motioning the princesses toward the Maypole. Slowly the reluctant group of girls moved toward the pole.

"I know this morning's events were a challenge,

and, uh, kind of smelly," Rapunzel began. "But you are a great bunch of princesses with a great deal of talent." She looked over the group in front of her.

"Lisette, the straw you spun this morning may have turned into butterscotch and not gold. But butterscotch is the right color . . . and it was delicious! And even though you didn't catch the Gingerbread Man, Gretel, you got back up after you tripped on the button he lost, and that showed determination!"

Snow noticed some of the princesses looking at one another — this was not the speech they expected, especially from Rapunzel.

"I just know that if we keep practicing and work together, we can win the Golden Ball!"

The girls were silent as they looked at one another doubtfully.

"We can do it!" shouted Antonella Printz, the Sash captain.

"Let's hear it for Princess School!" Astrid Glimmer added, clapping her hands over her head.

Tiffany Bulugia patted several of her fellow Robes on the back.

"Maybe we can," said a Sash quietly.

"I suppose it's possible," said a Crown.

Murmurs of hope began to move through the group. The princesses were finally ready to practice.

Within minutes, mock competitions were being played out all over the field. Josephine Crest made it through the Maze to Grandmother's House on her second try. Vishalia Lith actually hooked a unicorn-shoe around the spiral stake without hitting anyone. And Lisette Iderdown spun three pieces of straw into solid gold!

Rapunzel and the other captains moved from event to event, offering words of praise and encouraging the girls to keep practicing. Snow could tell that their new strategy was working. The teams were working hard, but also laughing and talking together. Snow sighed. She wished she felt like laughing, too.

"Okay, Hoppy," Snow said quietly to her Ball Fetch practice frog. "I would really love it if you could hop over to that spring and retrieve that ball for me."

"Ribbit, ribbit!" Hoppy replied. Then he quickly hopped off toward the water.

"How's your frog doing?" Ella called. She and Rose were at the next event over, tying their legs together with delicate ribbons of lace.

"Just fine!" Snow called back with a wave. But as she watched the small frog with a large wart on one side of his face hop back toward her, she felt a familiar icy chill run up her spine.

Snow looked around in alarm. She didn't expect to

see anything. She never did. But just then the sky darkened and a swarming flock of Grimm girls swooped down to the ground. They were here to practice!

No sooner had the witches landed than the cowering princesses from the morning returned as well. A group of Sashes huddled together on the edge of the Unicornshoes course, and a few Robes even ran into the maze to flee.

"Just ignore those nasty bats!" Rapunzel shouted. But nobody seemed to hear her — the princesses were too busy staring at the black-clad, pointy-hatted girls whose faces showed nothing but scorn.

"That's Hortense Hegbottom," Snow heard Rose whisper to Ella. Sure enough, Hortense was making a big show of stomping all over the field in her giant black boots, smashing every buttercup and dandelion.

"Are those cleats?" Goldilocks whispered to a girl next to her.

Snow shivered. Lucinta Pintch was staring at her through narrowed eyelids, and a chilling wind blew over the field.

Am I the only one who feels those cold gusts? Snow wondered. As she watched a large group of witches set up for Full Contact Maypole, she heard a whooshing sound overhead. A witch dressed from head to toe in silver and white was still flying in the sky. The hem of her dress was cut in jagged points that resembled icicles.

When she swooped low, Snow could see her strange, light-colored eyes, shiny like the blade of a sword.

"That's Violet Gust!" Eugenia Oak whispered, unable to keep the fear out of her voice. "She's won the Apple Bob for the last three years. When she's finished retrieving her apples, the water in the tub is like ice, and the drops on her face actually freeze!"

Snow wasn't sure if Eugenia was exaggerating or not, but just looking at Violet sent a whole new set of shivers up her spine. Though she hadn't said anything to her friends, the Apple Bob kept popping into her head. She was fascinated by it and knew there was no princess signed up to compete. But if Violet was involved, Snow knew she had better steer clear.

"Snow, you're shaking!" Rose said gently, coming up beside her and taking her friend's hand. "Don't worry. We're here with you."

Snow nodded, only slightly comforted by her friend's words. The princesses *were* standing together against the Grimms, but Malodora was only after *her*!

"Come on, everyone, back to practice!" Antonella called, herding the girls back to their various mock competitions. Still looking over their shoulders at the Grimms, the princesses resumed what they were doing before the witch flock landed.

Overhead, Violet swooped by again and again. Suddenly snow began to fall on the field!

Mayhem erupted almost immediately. The girls practicing Unicornshoes slipped when they threw, landing hard on their bustles. The princesses chasing the Gingerbread Man were sliding around so much they had no chance of catching the speeding cookie. Even Ella and Rose, usually a sure-footed Lace Race pair, tripped often on the icy ground.

Madame Garabaldi, the Bloomers' strict hearthroom teacher, emerged from one of the Princess School pavilions and crossed her arms over her chest. "Violet Gust!" she bellowed. "Come down here this instant!"

To Snow's surprise, Violet landed in front of the strict hearthroom teacher in less than two seconds.

"You know very well that magic is allowed neither at the Games nor the practices." Madame Garabaldi looked around at several other witches. "If I see any additional signs of magic or spells, you will forfeit the Golden Ball, per the rules set forth in the Maiden Games Regulations scroll."

Madame Garabaldi looked pointedly at both Violet and Hortense, who glared right back but remained silent.

"Now, I suggest you busy yourselves practicing," Madame Garabaldi finished. "The Games will be upon all of us shortly."

Snow watched as her teammates returned to practicing for the third time. Since Hoppy had already retrieved the ball for her, she decided to watch her friends for a few minutes. Rose's and Ella's legs were securely bound together with five pieces of lace, yet they moved around the course as gracefully as a single princess. Even in the face of a pair of heckling Grimm girls — one with a tremendous hooked nose and another with a humped back — they maintained an amazingly serene composure.

"I'd like to see the two of you *fly* with your legs tied together," Hooknose guffawed as she and her teammate tied their legs together to practice.

Rose and Ella ignored the taunt, but a moment later Ella's tiara started to slide off the top of her head. She caught it just in time, but reaching for it threw the girls off balance and they tumbled to the grass. Hump and Hook broke into a new fit of cackles.

"Can't you just take that thing off for practice?" Rose asked a little huffily.

"Uh, sure, I guess," Ella replied with a shrug. She took the tiara off and handed it to Snow. Without the distraction of the tiara, Ella became even more graceful, and she and Rose practically ran through the course. But before they got back to the finish line, a hoarse whisper echoed in Snow's ear.

"You must be Snow White," the voice hissed. "Headmistress Malodora is correct, as usual. You *are* as pale as ice."

Snow was so startled she nearly dropped Ella's tiara. Whirling around, she found herself face-to-face with Violet Gust herself.

"But you don't seem nearly as hard, or as sharp," Violet continued with a leer.

Snow was desperately searching for a reply when her friends were suddenly by her side, flanking her and forcing Violet to take a step back.

"Don't you have some practicing to do?" Ella asked.

"You must, since you won't be allowed to use your nasty magic," Rose added, looking Violet in the eye.

Violet's strange, sharp eyes glinted, and she turned up her pointed chin before flouncing off toward the Maypole.

Just before the end of the princesses' practice, the witches hopped on their broomsticks and swooped away like a murder of startled crows, leaving the princesses in peace. With the field to themselves, Astrid Glimmer and Antonella Printz brought out a giant tub from the equipment pavilion. It was filled with water, and several red apples bobbed on the surface.

"The Apple Bob has never been our competition," Antonella admitted to the group of girls that Rapunzel had gathered. "Princesses do not usually enjoy submerging their heads."

A low grumble rumbled through the crowd, and Snow knew why. *Usually* was an understatement. She had never met a single princess who would bob for an apple. Since the announcement of the Games, princesses had been gossiping about who might be willing to do it.

"Do we have a volunteer to try the first bob?" Antonella asked sheepishly.

"You love apples," Ella whispered to Snow. "Why don't you try it?"

Snow didn't respond. Her eyes were fixed on the round copper tub. She had to admit, the shiny fruits bobbing on top of the water were appealing. Slowly she got to her feet. Kneeling in front of the tub, she dove right in, soaking her entire head. A few seconds later she emerged with a shiny red apple in her teeth.

The princesses erupted with a rousing cheer. Snow was a natural. For the first time in years Princess School had a competitor for the Apple Bob!

Chapter Eleven
Games Day

The day of competition finally dawned. As Rose made her way to the stables, she admired the beautiful arena set on the grassy field beneath the pale morning sky. Over the past few days, school groundskeepers had transformed the practice field in honor of the Games.

There were now more than a dozen pavilions, each with colorful flags flying from its peaked corners. A long row of food booths took up one end of the field — some pink, gold, and purple, others gray, black, and a putrid green. While the novice princesses handed out fruit drinks and sweet and savory pastries, the Grimms offered newt stews and mud cocktails. The playing field was marked with lines showing where each competition would take place, with the Maypole at one end and the Maze to Grandmother's House at the other. The Gingerbread Man Chase took place on a trail that ran through and around various parts of the arena, and the judges' thronelike seats were lined up in a booth along the center of the field, where the more portable competitions would be held. Finally, at the edge of the field, looming over everything, was the Hall of Mirrors, a spooky exhibit prepared by the Grimm School each year.

Though some of the meeker princesses were too afraid, most dared to enter the Hall of Mirrors, and secretly enjoyed it. More or less like a maze, the Hall consisted of all kinds of mirrors that could make you look bigger, smaller, fatter, or taller . . . and multiplied visitors' reflections so that they appeared in several places at once. A few of the mirrors were even rumored to be enchanted.

Rose shivered as she walked past the Hall of Mirrors. She wasn't as spooked as she was excited. The entrance was shaped like the mouth of a giant, mythical beast — its jagged teeth nearly skimmed the heads of the girls who nervously stepped inside. Ever since she'd heard about the Grimms' tradition of setting it up for the Games, Rose had wanted to go see it for herself. But at the moment she didn't have time. She had promised Snow and Ella she'd meet them in the stables as soon as she arrived.

In the stables, Ella sat with a pale and shivering

Snow in a maize-colored stall. Rose tried not to frown when she saw that Ella was wearing her tiara. Didn't she *ever* take that thing off?

"She's here, and she knows I am, too," Snow said, her dark eyes brimming with tears.

Rose sat down and took Snow's hand. "There are loads of people out there," she said soothingly. "Malodora won't hurt you in a place this public."

"We'll stay with you the whole time," Ella added.

Snow wiped her cheeks and sighed. "I suppose I can't stay in here forever," she admitted. "Even though I'd like to." She looked at her friends, took a deep breath, and got to her feet.

Linking arms, the three girls headed out of the stables and onto the playing fields. Snow seemed a little shaky, but she put one foot in front of the other alongside Rose and Ella, and they made it to the arena.

"Did you see the Hall of Mirrors?" Rose asked as they walked past a row of food booths.

"I think it might be a good idea to steer clear of it," Ella said, gesturing with her head toward Snow.

One look at Snow's white-as-a-ghost face and Rose wanted to smack herself for even mentioning it. The last thing her friend needed was something else to scare her!

The girls approached the field just as the opening ceremony was ending. Rose would have liked to see it, but knew it would not have done Snow any good to hear her stepmother introduced. Now the Gingerbread Man Chase was about to begin. It was the first event to start, and often lasted the longest. Rose saw Rapunzel with the rest of the student captains at the starting line. She looked totally focused.

I just hope all our practicing pays off, Rose thought. Stepping between Snow and the judge's seats, Rose glanced toward the thrones. She spotted Malodora and Vermin Twitch immediately. Even at this distance, Rose noticed that Vermin's beady eyes and twitching nose made him look like a rodent. But he was nearly invisible next to Malodora. The woman commanded attention, and not in a pleasant way like Headmistress Bathilde. Malodora was dressed in a high-necked, long-sleeved black gown, with a full-length black cape that billowed behind her in the breeze, glinting purple in the sun. Her steely gaze studied the crowd intently, as if she was looking for something . . . or someone.

Rose steered her friends into a throng of princesses. The less visible Snow was, the better.

"Let's go see what's going on at Unicornshoes," she suggested.

"That's way at the end of the field!" Ella protested. "We don't want to be late for the Lace Race."

"We'll be back in plenty of time," Rose said as trumpeters blasted, announcing the beginning of the

81

Gingerbread Man Chase. While the wily cookie raced ahead, three witches and three princesses gave chase.

"I heard Rapunzel tell Gretel she couldn't have any sweets for two days before the competition," Ella giggled. "So she'd *really* want to catch him."

Indeed, Gretel was in the lead as the girls dashed after the elusive cookie. But the Gingerbread Man was notoriously fast.

"Go, Gretel!" Rose shouted.

The three girls cheered for their teammate until she disappeared into a thicket of trees. Then they headed over to Unicornshoes. Rapunzel was already there.

"You can do it, Ariel!" Rapunzel shouted loudly from the sidelines. The Grimms and the Princesses were neck and neck, with two shoes left to throw. If Ariel got both of them around the spiral horn, Princess School would win this competition.

A group of Grimms stood on the other side of the course, hissing and spitting at Ariel. Rose had to admire the way Ariel seemed to be ignoring them. If she was bothered by the witches' unsporting manners, she didn't show it. Her gaze never left the spiral horn as she swung her arm, tossing the heavy shoe into the air.

Ca-lunk! It ringed around the horn, then fell to the ground.

The cheering princesses clapped loudly while the witches hissed and booed.

Rapunzel jumped up and down. "Regal!" she shouted. Only one more to go!

Ariel's face showed intensity as she picked up another shoe. The Grimms snickered and hissed even more loudly, but Ariel seemed too focused to hear them. She stared at the spiral horn for a full minute, then threw the shoe.

"Too high!" Rapunzel whispered as the shoe left Ariel's hand. But at the last second the shoe dropped almost directly toward the ground, landing — *CLANK!* — around the horn. Princess School had won Unicornshoes!

The cheering was deafening as the girls congratulated one another with hugs. But a moment later trumpets sounded again. The next event — the Lace Race — was on deck.

"Let's get over there!" Rapunzel said, ushering Snow, Ella, and Rose toward the Lace Race.

"Okay, girls," Rapunzel said to Ella and Rose when they reached the starting line. "I know you're going to win this. Just don't lose concentration."

Rose helped Ella tie the ribbons of lace around their legs. Then, to Rose's relief, Ella handed her tiara to Snow. At least she wasn't going to let the tradition of wearing it ruin their chances of winning.

Ready to compete, Rose and Ella strode over and took their place at the starting line next to sneering

Humpback and Hooknose. The trumpet sounded three short blasts. They were off!

Like a seamless pair, Rose and Ella moved up the course, taking a fast lead. They were such a good match they didn't even need to pause to get in sync — they simply were.

Rose beamed as they slowed their pace a tiny bit to curve around the halfway marker. "We're doing great!" she whispered to Ella. But when she turned, something caught her eye: a group of cheering princesses, including many of the girls who were constantly crowded around Ella.

"El-la, El-la, El-la!" the girls cheered, jumping up and down.

Rose felt her face grow hot. Ella was only half of the team. What about her?

Anger bubbling up inside her, Rose couldn't take her eyes off the girls. And when her foot came down on an uneven section of grass, her ankle turned.

Rose had a split second to recover, but she was so angry, she didn't. She let herself — and Ella — fall instead.

Cackling madly, Hooknose and her teammate scuttled by and crossed the finish line.

While the Grimms chortled and cheered, Rapunzel scowled down at her friends.

"What happened?" she demanded. She glared at Rose. "It looked like you did that on purpose!"

More furious than ever — and partly at herself — Rose struggled to untangle her leg from Ella's.

"I don't know," Ella replied, sounding uncharacteristically angry. Her green eyes flashed at Rose. "Ask *her*."

"I guess you can't win all the time," Rose replied hotly.

"Neither can you, Rose," Ella snapped.

"And you!" Rose practically shouted, turning to Rapunzel. "Can't you think about anything besides winning? We could have been hurt!"

A long trumpet blare echoed across the field, signaling the next event: Ball Fetch. Rose finished untying herself from Ella and stood up.

"I don't have time for this," Rapunzel announced. "I need to get Snow ready for her event." For the first time the girls looked around for their friend.

Snow was nowhere to be found!

Chapter Twelve
Hide-and-Seek

Snow watched Ella and Rose gracefully stride forward, heading down the course with their legs tied together. Next to her, Rapunzel cheered loudly. Snow knew she should be cheering, too. But without Rose and Ella surrounding her, she suddenly felt exposed. She shuddered as the icy-cold feeling snaked up her spine — the fourth or fifth time since she'd woken up that morning. Malodora was watching her. Snow was sure if it. Snow stood stock-still, waiting for the awful feeling to pass. But it just kept getting stronger and stronger, until Snow was shivering in spite of the warm autumn sun.

"You can do it!" Rapunzel shouted, moving up the sidelines of the course. "Keep it smooth. And fast!"

Snow wrapped her cloak tightly around her with the hand that wasn't holding Ella's tiara. Nearby, a group of princesses began to chant Ella's name. "El-la,

El-la, El-la!" In the judges' booth, Malodora suddenly turned her attention toward the Lace Race.

Snow didn't waste any time. As soon as Rapunzel was a reasonable distance away, she fled toward the food booths. Shivering and with her heart racing, she searched for a place to hide.

"Would you like a little newt stew?" hissed a tall, thin witch with a crooked mouth.

Snow ignored her and rushed ahead, desperately searching for a tucked-away corner. Finally she spied a small space in between two booths.

Slumping down on the soft, green grass, Snow dropped the tiara and took a deep breath, waiting for her heartbeat to slow. Her head throbbed, and the memory of last night's nightmare roared through her mind.

She'd been trapped in Malodora's castle, in the dungeon, surrounded by jars of animal body parts and strange herbs. As she sat grinding frog bones into powder, her father's voice called out to her. The voice was everywhere at once, but Snow could not see him. Then Malodora's evil laugh echoed in the dim dungeon, and her father's voice disappeared altogether.

Snow gathered her blue cape around her, covering the sides of her head as she lay her forehead on her knees. She wished more than anything that she could disappear. Her head throbbed mercilessly, and the screaming crowd made her eyes ache. She heard the awful sound of Grimm girls roaring with excitement. Snow lifted her head to listen. Could the Grimms have won the Lace Race?

Snow was barely aware of time passing as she sat between the food booths, wishing the Games were over. And then familiar voices — friendly ones — were suddenly moving in her direction. Looking up, Snow saw Rose, Ella, and Rapunzel standing over her.

Ella sat down immediately, throwing her arms around Snow. "We're so glad you're all right," she cried. "What happened?"

Snow's dark eyes glistened as she gazed at her friends. "I just felt so awful, so exposed out there," she said. "And then that icy feeling came over me. I just had to . . . to get away," she sobbed.

"We lost the Lace Race," Ella said, shooting a not-so-friendly look at Rose.

Snow wiped away a tear. "I thought I heard the Grimms cheering," she said. "How did it happen?"

"We don't have time to talk about that now," Rapunzel said. "We need to get you to your first event, Snow. The Ball Fetch is about to start."

Just then the trumpets sounded, and the girls heard the last call for the Ball Fetch.

Snow's eyes widened. "I . . . I can't," she said. "Malodora will see me."

"We'll stay with you the whole time, Snow," Rose said softly. "We're finished with our event, so we don't have to leave your side for a second."

"I know it's a lot to ask," Rapunzel admitted. "But your team really needs you. We have to win the Fetch if we're going to have a chance at winning the Golden Ball."

Snow was silent for several long seconds.

"Please, Snow?" whispered Ella as she picked up her tiara and placed it on her head.

Snow sniffled, then looked up. "All right," she said. "I'll do it for the three of you."

"That's the spirit!" Rapunzel crowed, already backing away. "I have to get back to the field. But I'll see you over at the competition."

Snow nodded and tried to smile as Rapunzel sped off. Rose and Ella helped Snow to her feet. Snow steeled herself as her friends led her out onto the open field.

Just one step at a time, she told herself as they began to cross the arena. But she could not keep her eyes from darting toward the judges' booth, where Malodora sat surveying the field like a hungry hawk. Her eyes swept the field in one direction, then moved back toward the area where Snow and her friends were.

Snow inhaled sharply and stopped in her tracks like a mouse trying to avoid capture.

"What's wrong?" Rose asked, trying to lead Snow forward.

"Keep moving, Snow," Ella encouraged. "When my stepmother is mean to me, I always try to keep moving."

Snow allowed her friends to pull her forward, but it took every ounce of her will to do so.

I promised, she told herself. *I said I would do the Ball Fetch.*

Finally the girls reached the Ball Fetch area, where Rapunzel was offering a few words of encouragement to the other competing princesses. Half a dozen frogs were lined up, croaking excitedly as they waited for the race to begin.

Rose and Ella led Snow to her position at the starting line. Rapunzel was by Snow's side in a minute.

"Okay, Snow," she said quietly. "They held the start. Now all you have to do is ask Croaky to fetch the ball from the spring for you."

Snow gazed down at Croaky, who seemed to be smiling up at her. Usually such a sight would make Snow feel better. It didn't.

"Why is this taking so long?" boomed a voice from the judges' booth. Malodora. This time the icy shiver sank into Snow's shoulders like talons and snaked its way down her spine, overtaking her completely.

I can't do it! Snow screamed in her head. With one last fleeting look at Croaky, she scrambled to her feet and tore away from the starting line.

Chapter Thirteen
A Slim Victory

For a moment Ella was too surprised to move. She just stood there watching Snow disappear into the crowd, leaving her, Rose, and Rapunzel at the Ball Fetch starting line.

Finally Ella snapped out of it. "I'm going after her!" she announced.

Rapunzel put her hand on Ella's shoulder. "Let me," she said in her serious coach voice. "I need you and Rose to stay here and take Snow's place in the Fetch. Somebody's got to convince Croaky to get that ball."

Ella shook Rapunzel's arm off. Snow had run off faster than a spooked horse, and Ella was really worried.

Besides, she thought, stealing a look at Rose, who avoided her eyes, *the last thing I want to do after the Lace Disgrace is another competition with Rose.* Ella had no idea what the problem was, but Rose was all thorns.

Ella was about to say something when Rapunzel

stopped her. She put one hand on each of her friends' shoulders. "You and Rose are the perfect team — or at least you *can* be. I'll find Snow, then I have to get ready for Maypole. You two can do this."

"Ella doesn't need me," Rose said as she got to her feet. "I'll go look for Snow." Without waiting for a reply, Rose slipped out from under Rapunzel's hand and disappeared in the crowd.

Ella was speechless again. What was going on with her friends?

For a second, Rapunzel looked as shocked as Ella felt. Then she turned, and without a word gave Ella a look before taking off after Rose and Snow. There was no mistaking Rapunzel's meaning. Somebody had to stay and do the Fetch. And that somebody was Ella.

Sighing, Ella looked at the dampish green frog and wished she was the one who had to coax Snow out of hiding instead of this amphibian into fetching. Croaky nabbed a fly with his long, sticky tongue. He had a big belly and looked more interested in a nap than a swim in the spring. Sure, any frog would swim to the bottom of the spring for Snow White. There was just something about Snow that made every creature want to do its best for her — its very best. Well, her best was all Ella could do now.

Lined up at the starting line were five other frogs with girls standing behind them. Suddenly a trumpet blasted, startling Ella, and the other girls crouched down to start convincing their frogs to do their bidding. Ella got on her hands and knees and looked into Croaky's yellow eyes.

"Okay, Croaky," Ella tried to sound firm like Rapunzel and sweet like Snow at the same time. "It's just you, me, and the ball. Let's get it together."

The frog looked back at Ella blankly. He definitely did not look inspired. But then, to Ella's surprise, he leaped off — in the *right* direction!

Croaky was first off the block! Soon the rest of the frogs started hopping, too. Most of them were faster than Croaky and the gap between them narrowed. In no time Lucinta Pintch's large frog was taking the lead, but Croaky took a big leap and landed just ahead of the beefier bullfrog.

On the sidelines a particularly grungy witch furiously scratched at her tangled hair, sending a shower of tiny bugs and moths raining down on the grass. Her friends snickered and nudged her with their sharp elbows. She was trying to distract the frogs with the little insects. And it was working!

Croaky paused to gulp down a mealworm. Another frog competing for Princess School took off in the wrong direction. Lucinta's frog, Bump, was in the lead!

Satisfied with his snack, Croaky hopped back into the race, but he was at least two leaps behind Bump.

"Go, little green guy! You can do it!" Ella encouraged him even though her own hope of winning was fading. Bump's leaps were nearly twice as long as Croaky's. But who knew what would happen when Croaky got to the spring? Maybe he could swim better than he could hop.

It looked like the race was over when Bump suddenly slowed. He was tracking a moth that had fluttered over his head.

Beside Ella, Lucinta jumped up and down on her stick legs, screaming angrily. "You lumpy, bumpy sack of warts! Get in there and get that ball or I'll use your tongue in my next batch of brew!"

Lucinta's frog snapped the moth out of the air and chewed slowly.

"Go!" Lucinta screamed. "Or your tadpoles are toast!"

Bump didn't seem to hear or care. Satisfied with his moth meal, he stayed just where he was, closing his eyes for a little rest.

The Grimm girls' jeering cheers turned to hisses when Croaky hit the water. It looked like he was going to be the winner. Ella looked around for a moment, wishing her friends could see this. Across the field she saw Rapunzel getting ready for Full Contact Maypole. Rapunzel looked back at Ella and shook her head. She hadn't found anyone. *Where was Snow?*

Ella used the time Croaky was submerged to scan the crowd. She saw hundreds of faces, some gnarled and some lovely. But Snow's sweet, pale face was not among them. Not even in the bleachers . . .

Ella looked at the stands again and felt a fleeting hope. All seven of Snow's dwarves were there, waving pink-and-purple Princess School banners. Nod was asleep, his head hanging over the back of his seat. His banner fluttered each time he exhaled, tickling Wheezer's nose and making him sneeze even more uncontrollably than usual. Meek spotted Ella and waved shyly. Ella's heart sank again when she realized for certain that Snow was not with them.

Then Ella noticed something else. In the judges' booth someone was missing. Malodora's throne was empty!

Ella's heart raced. She was terrified for Snow. She had to tell someone, but couldn't leave her spot. Croaky was still diving and more frogs were hitting the water.

Finally Croaky's green head broke the surface. He held a golden ball firmly in his mouth. Proudly he flopped out of the water and spat the ball toward Ella's feet. They'd won! Princesses were jumping up and down all around Ella, circling her and cheering. They didn't understand that she didn't have time for celebrating, and she wasn't in the mood. She was too scared for her friends . . . all of them.

Chapter Fourteen

True Reflections

How do you find someone when you feel lost yourself? Rose wondered. All around her, girls were hurrying toward the noisy crowds already swarming around the Ball Fetch and the Maypole. Rose searched for signs of Snow's dark hair and red lips. She didn't see her, but suspected Snow would be headed in the other direction, anyway — away from the crowd.

Away, she thought. *That's where I'd like to be, too.*

Rose could not remember a time when she'd felt so confused. Usually she knew just what was going on and what to do next. Right now she felt like giving up completely. Girl after girl pushed past her. Grisly Grimm girls sneered at the perfect-looking princess. Some of Rose's classmates smiled. Still there was no sign of Snow.

This is useless! Rose's feelings of defeat turned to

rage in her head, then back to desperation. *What is wrong with me? Even if I find Snow, how will I be any help?*

When she reached the edge of the field, the sound of cheering girls started to fade into the background. Before her stretched an open grinning mouth: the Hall of Mirrors. Rose was drawn closer toward the entrance.

I just need a minute to think, she told herself as she stepped inside.

Though the light within the cavernous pavilion was dim, the reflections in the many mirrors were dazzling. Multiple Roses gazed back at the true Rose, reflecting her lost expression again and again.

"You don't look like you have any answers!" Rose told one image. "And you!" She turned to scold herself in another mirror. "What are you looking at? You aren't helping anyone by just thinking of yourself, you know." Rose stared at her reflection as the words she had just spoken sank in. Their unvarnished truth stung Rose and tears sprang to her eyes.

Following the path toward larger and more distorted images, Rose let the tears come. She felt sorry for herself, but most of all she felt foolish. At last she understood what she was feeling. It was jealousy. She was jealous of Ella! She was so accustomed to getting all the attention and feeling annoyed with it, that she never expected to be upset when the spotlight shone on someone else.

Am I really so shallow? Rose wondered. She gazed at herself in a huge gold-framed looking glass that made her appear as flat as a carpet. *Am I really going to let this stupid jealousy ruin one of the best friendships I've ever had, and the whole school's chances of winning the Golden Ball?*

Rose stared steadily into a new mirror. She did not like what she saw and she was ready to do something about it. She'd thrown the Lace Race and deserted the Ball Fetch. Even if Princess School still managed to win the Fetch, winning the Maypole *and* the Apple Bob would be crucial.

I'll find Snow, Rose thought. *I'll stop thinking about myself and be a good friend.* But first she had to find her way out of the mirrored hall.

It didn't seem like she had walked very far into the Hall of Mirrors, but as Rose turned corner after corner she didn't see any shafts of light to indicate that the edges of the canvas pavilion were near. Her heart was beginning to race when she came around another bend and saw something that made it stop beating altogether. Malodora!

Rose flattened herself against a wall and peeked around the corner to make sure she hadn't just seen another mirror trick.

She hadn't. Malodora was real.

The evil queen was standing in front of a huge mirror with her arms raised. Her midnight-purple sleeves hung so low they nearly touched the floor. Malodora was murmuring something to herself.

Slowly Malodora lowered her arms. Rose watched as the image in the mirror swirled and changed. Clouds bloomed and disappeared. Lightning flashed. No, wait. That wasn't lightning. It was flashes of light reflected in a tiny fissure crack.

In the mist that swirled on the mirror's surface, Rose thought she could make out a face.

Then a voice boomed, "What may I show you, my queen?"

Malodora's throaty voice echoed eerily in the chamber.

> *Magic mirror before me,*
> *I sense Snow White, but cannot see.*
> *Tell me true where she doth dwell*
> *that I may cast my evil spell.*

When she finished speaking, Malodora held her chin high and waited impatiently for an answer.

Rose shook her head. She felt like she was waking from a nightmare. Only this nightmare was real. Snow was in serious danger. If Rose didn't find her before Malodora did . . .

Rose gasped. She couldn't imagine what would happen!

There was no time to waste. Not waiting to hear what the magic mirror would say, Rose turned as quickly and quietly as she could. She ran two steps, and then — CRASH! Her petticoats caught on the mirror behind her, pulling it over. It shattered into a million shards and exposed her to the witch!

Frozen in her tracks, Rose cringed, preparing for the worst. Malodora spun once. Glaring at Rose, she silently lifted her hand. She pointed one daggerlike fingernail directly at Rose. With her other arm, she raised her cloak and brought it swooping down over her head. In a puff of smoke she was gone.

Rose didn't wait for the smoke to clear. She ran full speed, unsure of where she was going. The Hall felt darker, and all around her, figures loomed. She could hear the cackles of Grimm witches echoing everywhere.

Suddenly she came to a dead end. When she turned around, the path she had come down was gone! Mirrors closed her in on all sides. Her reflection was distorted infinitely in every direction.

Awful pinched faces danced in the glass — Lucinta and Violet! The witches taunted her in the smooth glass, sticking out their tongues, wagging their knobby fingers, and cackling maliciously. Rose turned again and again, trying to escape their gaze.

Their faces were too awful to look at — cruel, drawn mouths, green-tinted skin, and nasty eyes. With a jolt, Rose realized the hideous faces in the mirror had changed. Now she was looking at her own green reflection. *She* was a witch!

Rose screamed. A crack zigzagged down one of the mirrors and a new image appeared. It was Snow! She was okay! Rose felt relief wash over her as she watched an image of herself standing with Snow in the sunlight. Holding a juicy-looking apple, Snow smiled sweetly. She opened her mouth for a bite, but the moment the apple touched her mouth Snow fell to the ground and lay completely still.

Rose sank to her knees and hid her face in her hands. "No!" she screamed.

But there was no answer, only silence and reflections she was too frightened to look at.

Chapter Fifteen
Finding Courage

Snow cautiously peeked out at the playing field from underneath the shiny white bleachers. She could see Rapunzel gripping the satin Maypole ribbon tightly in her hand. Rapunzel crouched low to the ground and gave the Grimm witch in front of her a look that Snow recognized: Rapunzel meant business.

Snow couldn't blame her. Even in her terrified state she knew the Maiden Games competition had been fierce. Princess School was still in it to win, but Snow knew if they didn't take Full Contact Maypole, it would all be over for the royals.

"Sprat!" a humpbacked witch snarled at her long-nosed teammate. "You take 'Sparkly' over there and I'll get 'Moldylocks.'" The stooped witch motioned with her pointed chin — first to Astrid and then to Rapunzel.

Snow felt her stomach turn, but Rapunzel didn't even acknowledge the witch's words.

She's probably focusing every bit of her energy on winning, Snow thought admiringly. Rapunzel was the bravest person she knew, and an amazing competitor. Snow, on the other hand, was a coward. She'd run away from Ball Fetch, letting her whole school down!

When the trumpets blasted, Snow could tell that Rapunzel was ready. Eight witches holding ribbons began their counterclockwise charge toward Rapunzel and the other princesses. Snow winced as she witnessed the toughness of the game. This was not like Delicate Touch!

The princesses did not shrink or cower. They stepped lightly and quickly around the witches with their heads held high. But the Grimms were playing dirty.

On one side of the pole, Hortense Hegbottom heaved herself up to stomp on Tiffany's ribbon, shredding and grinding it into the mud. Tiffany was out. A second witch lunged past a princess and then turned and hissed, scaring the princess so badly she dropped her ribbon. It fluttered limply to the grass. That princess was out, too.

Snow could tell that the Grimm strategy was to intimidate the princesses, while the princesses were going for speed. Snow remembered Rapunzel coaching the girls to stay away from the Grimms as much as possible and to focus on circling the pole. "Avoid direct confrontation," she'd told them. But Snow could tell Rapunzel's strategy wasn't working.

Quickly Rapunzel stopped circling the pole and stayed in one place, blocking witches and helping the other princesses make it around. She was thinking on her feet, Snow realized, changing the strategy.

For a moment Snow thought the new plan was really helping. With a leap, Rapunzel jumped over a Grimm girl who had tucked herself into a cannonball aimed right for Rapunzel's legs. Reaching out, Rapunzel hooked the witch's ribbon and pulled it from her grasp. Hump was out.

But so were five princesses! Everything was coming unraveled. Snow could see Rapunzel quickly sizing up the situation and deciding what to do. A second later she started moving again. She met Sprat with a classic skip-trip. Rapunzel made it past, but Sprat kept her ribbon, too.

Dodging and weaving like a jackrabbit, Rapunzel made it four times around the pole without looking up. Snow held her breath. Rapunzel and Astrid were the only princesses still in the game, pitted against four witches!

Make that five. Snow spotted Hortense and her monster boots barreling full speed at Rapunzel. Rapunzel spun to the inside and crashed headlong into Sprat, taking a bony elbow to the shin. Sprat sniggered, but Astrid was there, catching the witch off guard and slipping the ribbon from her hands with a small curtsy.

104

It was a majestic move, but there was no time for compliments. Side by side, Rapunzel and Astrid wound their way around the pole, facing each new assault as a team. It looked as though they would *both* finish when Rapunzel saw Hortense coming at them like a speeding boulder with teeth.

Rapunzel stepped ahead of Astrid to bear the brunt of Hortense's assault, but the witch stepped aside at the last moment. Astrid stumbled. And just as she fell, Hortense raised a massive boot to stomp on her competitor.

There was nothing Rapunzel could do. You could not turn around and go the other way in Maypole. Luckily, Astrid rolled away just as Hortense's spikes came down. The princess was spared, but her ribbon was lost.

Snow could barely watch. Alone on the field Rapunzel picked up speed. She only had to make it around the pole one more time to win the game. But it wouldn't be easy.

The four remaining Grimm girls focused their evil sneers on Rapunzel and formed a wall of witches. They stopped moving and stood waiting to rip Rapunzel's ribbon from her hand.

Smiling back at them, Rapunzel rounded the pole. She may have been just one girl on the field, but she had grace and agility on her side. And she had something else. Nearly every girl in Princess School was watching, cheering her on. Snow felt sure she was the only princess not yelling!

Snow could almost see the cheering bolster Rapunzel's courage. She stood taller and looked Hortense straight in the eyes. Watching her, Snow felt full of pride. Her friend would not be intimidated!

With a final burst of speed, Rapunzel feinted right, crouched low, and jumped! The witches tried to move as one and tripped. When they attempted to leap and block they all went in different directions, bumping heads and tangling themselves in a mass of ribbons and limbs.

While the Grimms lay on the field hissing and spitting at one another like a ball of writhing snakes, Rapunzel skipped the rest of the way around the pole and finished her lap with a twirl and a bow to the judges. The crowd went wild.

In the judge's box, Vermin Twitch held a megaphone to the end of his quivering snout. "Full Contact Maypole goes to Princess School," he announced flatly in his nasal voice, clearly not very excited. Beside him, a scowling Malodora took her seat.

Snow longed to run from her hiding place and give Rapunzel the hug she deserved. But Malodora was so close she dared not move.

Snow watched Rapunzel look around, searching

for her friends. But before she could spot them she was swept up in a giant hug by her Maypole team-mates.

"We won the Ball Fetch!" Snow heard Astrid yell over the cheers. "If we can just win the Gingerbread Man and the Apple Bob, the Golden Ball will be ours!"

Rapunzel smiled back at Astrid, while under the bleachers two tears trickled down Snow's frozen face. Princess School was so close to taking the Maiden Games — but they would not. And it was all her fault.

Chapter Sixteen
Searching for Snow

"You did it!" Ella joined the pack of princesses hugging Rapunzel. She had run from the Ball Fetch to the Maypole as quickly as she could and had managed to see Rapunzel's victory lap.

"So did you!" Rapunzel was flushed with excitement. She hugged Ella back. "We won!"

"You trounced those witches!" Val appeared out of nowhere. He clapped Rapunzel on the back and tousled her bangs as if she were his jousting steed.

Rapunzel shook him off. "Thanks." She grinned. "It's about time you showed up. Where have you been?" she teased.

"Some of us attend classes during the school day. We don't have time for silly games." Val clicked his heels together, stood up straight, and lifted his nose in the air as if he was trying to smell something distant and not at all pleasant. But he couldn't hold the snobbish stance for long. His smile returned and he leaned closer to Rapunzel and Ella. "Actually, I let Hans Charming best me in fencing so I could sit out and sneak away early. It wasn't easy — Hans can't fence his way out of a coach!"

Ella laughed. Val's eyes were shining. Obviously he was enjoying the win as much as Rapunzel. And even Ella.

Ella had to admit it felt good to win the Fetch — much better than it had losing the Lace Race with Rose. But the thought of Rose — and Snow — brought Ella back to reality.

Rapunzel seemed to read Ella's mind. "The Games aren't over yet," she said, getting serious.

"Do you know where Snow is?" Ella asked.

"I was hoping she was with Rose," Rapunzel replied.

Ella pinched her lips together. "I suppose she could be, but I don't know where Rose is, either."

"Rose is missing?" Val asked, sounding alarmed.

Rapunzel ignored the prince and scanned the crowd. The swarms around the Maypole were beginning to drift away to other parts of the field. "They should be back by now." Rapunzel squinted into the distance. "Unless something happened . . ."

"Malodora wasn't in her box during the Fetch," Ella said, suddenly remembering. Fear shook her voice.

"We have to find Snow. Now." Rapunzel was getting good at giving orders. And Ella was happy to follow them.

"Let's split up," Rapunzel continued. But before she could point Ella in a direction, the Robe captain, Tiffany Bulugia, made a quick curtsy and cut in.

"Rapunzel! Rapunzel! We need you over here!" Tiffany pulled Rapunzel by the arm. She was talking fast. "It's the Gingerbread Man. The competition has been going on for hours. The princesses are running and running as fast as they can, but two of them have fainted from exhaustion!"

Ella watched as Rapunzel was pulled away. Rapunzel glanced back. The look in her eyes was pained.

"Go help the team," Ella yelled. "We'll take care of Snow!"

"And Rose!" Val added with a wave.

Now it was Ella's turn to give orders. "You take that side, I'll take this." She pointed. "Snow won't want to be found, so check *everywhere*."

Val nodded and bowed. Ella didn't wait to see him flourish his hat before she started peeking into every dark corner she could find in the arena. Snow wasn't anywhere. Ella was beginning to lose hope when, crouching low and peering under the bleachers, she heard a sniff. She ducked lower and spotted a pale white elbow. Snow!

Ella crawled beneath the bleachers to join her frightened friend. "Are you okay?" she asked gently.

"They need me." Snow sniffed. "I'm the only one who can do the Apple Bob." The pale girl shook and talked in a whisper. "I want to do it, Ella. But I just can't stand to have my stepmother's eyes on me. I just . . . freeze."

Ella laid her arm across Snow's trembling shoulders. She knew what it felt like to be frightened, but she had never been so scared she couldn't move. "You don't have to do anything, Snow. These are just games. You matter to us more than winning." As she spoke, Ella knew her words were true.

Snow sniffed. "I want to do it, Ella. I really do."

Ella smiled weakly at Snow. She wanted to help her, but how could she give her friend courage?

Suddenly she spotted some familiar red shoes walking past the bottom row of seats. She stuck out her hand and grabbed Red's ankle. Red shrieked.

"Shhh!" Ella hissed.

Red crouched down and looked into the shadows under the seats. "Ella!" She smiled. "Snow!"

"Shhhh!" Ella and Snow hissed in unison, and Ella pulled the cloaked girl under the bleachers with them.

"What is it?" Red whispered. "Are you in trouble? Is it a wolf? Do you need me to call a huntsman?"

"No, nothing like that," Ella explained. "We just need to borrow your riding cape."

"This old thing?" Red asked, shrugging off the large, hooded cloak she always wore. "Gladly! My mother makes me wear this thing everywhere. My real name isn't even 'Red,' you know. It's Scarlet. People started —"

"Thanks," Ella interrupted, taking the cape and pulling it around Snow's shoulders. Red was really nice, but boy, could she talk!

"Oh, that looks good on you!" Red cooed when Ella pulled the hood around Snow's face. "Red is your color! You look totally different. I almost don't recognize you!"

"Perfect," Ella said softly.

Snow managed a weak smile. Beneath her hands Ella felt Snow stop shaking.

"Ready?" she asked.

From deep in the hood, Ella heard Snow's soft, sweet voice.

"Ready."

Chapter Seventeen

Bobbing for Apples

Snow took one small step at a time as she and Ella made their way toward the apple-bobbing area. The Bob would take place right in front of the judges' booth since it was the final event. As they approached, Snow could feel the icy fingers grasping her neck, and her feet slowed. It was only because of Ella's reassuring hand on her arm and the cloak disguise that she kept moving at all.

This hood may not keep Malodora from seeing me, Snow thought, *but it keeps me from seeing her.* Peeking out cautiously, Snow spotted Rapunzel by one of the copper bobbing tubs. At first Rapunzel didn't recognize Snow. She kept glancing around the field with a worried expression. But as they got closer Snow saw a smile spread across Rapunzel's face and she stepped away from the tub to meet them.

"I'm so glad you're all right," she whispered to

Snow. "And that you're here. You can do this, Snow. I just know it."

Snow wished she felt as sure as her friend sounded. As Ella led her over to her apple tub, she seemed to be looking around for someone. It didn't take Snow long to figure out who — Rose. Where was she?

A moan from the Princess School side of the crowd interrupted Snow's thoughts.

"They must really think you're Red," Rapunzel whispered excitedly. "And if they can't tell it's you, the witches won't be able to, either." A sly smile spread across her face. "This could be our biggest secret weapon yet!"

Snow wanted to share in her friend's pleasure, but for some reason she didn't. Unable to help herself, she stole a glance at Malodora. The queen's piercing light blue eyes ran over her like an icy shower, causing Snow to shiver. But a moment later her gaze fell on something else in the stands — the dwarves! They were holding handmade signs, and some of them were waving them like banners in the air. GO SNOW! read Nod's. Only Nod was fast asleep, leaning against a very put-out-looking Gruff. Only the letters OW in the SNOW of Nod's sign were actually legible.

Snow giggled. Her surrogates must have taken the afternoon off to come and cheer her on. And they had even made signs! Meek and Wheezer were laughing and pointing to the Gingerbread Man, who had been caught by a princess but was now being chased again by a very hungry Gretel.

POUNCE, PRINCESSES! declared the sign held in Hap's stubby fingers. Hap and Dim watched the apple-bobbing area with great interest. Mort held his hand over his eyes and peered intently at the field.

Are they looking for me? Snow guessed that they were. And she felt terrible for not really being there . . . even though she was. She watched Hap lift his sign as high as he could, which was barely above the heads of the spectators in front of him. The dwarves may have been small of frame, but they had huge hearts. And they loved her.

"You can do this, Snow," Ella whispered. "We'll be right here with you."

Snow felt the icy feeling drain from her limbs, replaced by a wonderful warmth. It spread from her torso to her fingers and toes. Suddenly Snow knew that she really *could* do it. Her head no longer ached, and for the first time in weeks she felt sure of herself and of what she needed and wanted to do. And no one was going to stop her. Not even Malodora.

Taking a deep breath, Snow stepped away from her supportive friends and lowered the red hood. She was tired of hiding.

"It's Snow White!" came the whispers from the

115

crowd. And within seconds the whispers were replaced by resounding cheers. The dwarves cheered louder than anyone. "Hey, ho, there's our Snow!"

"Go, Snow!" princesses shouted.

The Grimm girls hissed loudly, glaring at Snow White. From her judge's throne, Malodora continued to stare at Snow coldly. But the edges of her cruel mouth twisted upward in the tiniest hint of a smile.

Snow ignored Malodora completely as she stepped up to her bobbing tub. Thirteen shiny apples danced on the surface.

Her heart racing, Snow waited for the trumpet to sound. She was ready when the blast came, lowering her head toward the water's surface with lightning speed.

Snow pulled out her first apple in fewer than five seconds, then her second and her third. Every ounce of her being was focused on the apples in the tub in front of her. Her whole body tingled with exhilaration. Next to her, Violet the bobbing Grimm witch was retrieving apples just as quickly. The two girls were neck and neck.

Faster, Snow told herself. *You've got to get them faster.*

Behind her, the crowd was cheering like crazy. She heard Hap's voice as she threw herself forward again, trapping an apple against the bottom of the tub almost immediately. After sinking her teeth into the crisp flesh, she came up for air. When she pulled her head out of the bucket, cold water splashed down the front of her dress. Snow ignored it.

"Hey, ho! Go, Snow!" the dwarves cheered in singsong unison.

Snow smiled to herself when the sound of their cheerful voices reached her ears. She was still stunned that they had taken a day off from work to watch the games — to watch *her*. But she had to stay focused on the apples. . . .

Suddenly a strange feeling came over her. The dwarves' voices seemed to fade, and her gaze fell on one particular apple bobbing on the side of the bucket — an apple with one white side and one red one that Snow hadn't noticed before. The apple glinted in the sun. Snow could not take her eyes off it. She had to have that apple.

Chapter Eighteen
Mirror, Mirror

Rose slumped against one of the mirrors that made up her mirror cage and let out another sob. Everything seemed so hopeless. Snow was in trouble, and she was trapped in some kind of cursed reflective cage. Images swam before her — Lucinta's and Violet's sneering faces, Malodora's gnarled, daggerlike fingernail, Snow falling lifeless to the ground, her own desperate face. Malodora's chant echoed in her head, again and again like a broken gramophone.

Magic mirror before me,
I sense Snow White, but cannot see.
Tell me true where she doth dwell
that I may cast my evil spell.

Rose pulled her knees to her chest and lay her head upon them, hoping to shut out the horrible images.

But they played over and over again behind her closed eyelids. There was no escaping them.

Another sob escaped Rose's chest. How could she warn her friend if she couldn't even get out?

Lucinta's high-pitched cackle rang so loudly in her ears Rose thought her skull would shatter. She was about to scream when something caused her to look up instead — a noise.

Was that the screaming crowd? Were those princesses cheering, or witches? Rose couldn't tell.

I have to be calm, Rose told her reflection as she wiped away tears with the sleeve of her gown. *If I don't, I definitely won't be able to help myself, or my friends.*

My friends, she repeated, closing her eyes. She could still hear the jeering laughter of Lucinta and Violet, but she ignored it as she pictured the smiling faces of her friends. The straightforward, headstrong Rapunzel. The warm, friendly Ella. And the sweet, always cheerful Snow. Before she came to Princess School, Rose had never really had friends, only admirers. Now there was a group of girls she could trust and confide in, count on for anything.

Rose looked at the mirror before her again. Her distorted reflection was still there. But this time Lucinta and Violet were gone. Rose was surrounded by her friends and they were all smiling at her, giving her strength.

Reaching out, Rose placed both hands on one of the mirrors that made up her cage. She pushed — hard — and it fell backward to the floor, smashing to a hundred pieces. And as the last shard of reflective glass landed on the floor with a quiet ping, the voices of Lucinta and Violet were silenced.

Carefully Rose stepped over the shattered glass and quickly made her way down the exposed corridor. She could hear the sounds of the Maiden Games coming from the arena. She walked toward the noise, letting it guide her. The sound was initially reassuring. She felt hope building. She could still make it out in time! But then she heard a chorus calling Snow's name, and she realized that the Apple Bob had already begun. Panic filled her heart and she started to run. Left, right, left. The Hall of Mirrors seemed endless. There had to be a way out!

At last she spotted a sliver of light through a flapping tent door. Gasping for breath, she raced toward it as the sound of the crowd got louder. By the time Rose surged into the daylight it was roaring in her ears, along with her own single thought:

Please don't let me be too late!

Chapter Nineteen
The Enchanted Apple

"Hey, ho. We love Snow!" cheered the dwarves in the stands.

Snow shook her head, and water drops flew from her dark locks. She ignored the red-and-white apple on the far side of the bucket and dunked her head to retrieve another apple nearby. All around her, her friends and family were cheering madly. The noise was deafening, but she was focused on the task in front of her.

Snow went after each apple like a cat chasing a scurrying mouse. She'd pulled out so many apples she'd lost count — eight, maybe nine — at least as many as Violet Gust beside her. Snow's brow furrowed as she imagined the icy witch beside her. She would not let Violet beat her. She was out to win.

But as she leaned forward, again her attention was drawn to the strange apple she'd noticed before.

It's on the edge, Snow told herself. *Get the others first and then go for that one.*

Still it pulled at her. Gritting her teeth, Snow ignored the odd apple and dove in, pinning an all-red one in less than three seconds.

"Hey, ho, that's our Snow!" the dwarves whooped in the stands, getting to their feet to dance a little jig. With Rapunzel and Ella leaping like gazelles behind her, Snow retrieved another apple, pulling ahead of Violet.

"You can do it, Snow!" Ella screamed at the top of her lungs.

Snow's entire body was filled with exhilaration. She was doing it! She was going to win! And she was standing up to Malodora, something she never thought she'd have the courage to do!

Snow stole a glance at Violet and could almost taste victory. Violet's apple pile looked smaller than hers! But as she lowered her head to dive again, Snow's stomach lurched with sudden hunger, and her eyes locked on the strange apple bobbing enticingly at the tub's edge. All of a sudden it seemed to be the only one that could satisfy her appetite. Her head spun, and everything shifted out of focus. She felt dizzy. Confused. But more than anything else, she felt hungry. She had to have that apple.

Snow dove, chasing the strange apple straight to

the bottom of the copper tub. Where was it? She could feel its presence, but couldn't find it with her mouth. She opened her eyes under water, but the water was so churned up it was impossible to see clearly. She raised her head.

"Snow!" Rapunzel shouted. "Hurry! She's catching up!"

"Come on, Snow!" Ella screamed desperately.

Snow heard her friends' words, but could not pull her focus away from that apple. Hunger was gnawing at her stomach — at the very core of her being. And then there was another voice, even louder than Rapunzel and Ella, and more frantic. The voice screamed a single word: "NOOOOOO!"

Diving deep, Snow pinned the half-red, half-white apple to the bottom. She sank her teeth into the crisp flesh. She felt a moment of complete victory. But an instant later she seemed to lose control of her body. She felt her torso and limbs jerk up mechanically, sending water flying everywhere. Staring at but not seeing the confused crowd, she stood for a second with the apple clenched in her teeth. Then she crumpled to the field in a heap as the apple rolled to the sidelines, and everything went black.

Chapter Twenty
Fairest in the Land

The next few minutes felt like an eternity. Rapunzel watched it all happen in slow motion. Snow jerked upright, flinging her drenched head back on her shoulders and spraying water everywhere. For a second she stood and seemed triumphant. The trumpets blasted, signaling the end of the Apple Bob just as Rose raced into the center of the Bob arena, screaming.

"Nooo!" Rose's scream nearly drowned out the trumpets. All eyes were on her. Then Snow crumpled to the grass, lifeless.

Rapunzel was too stunned to move. She and Ella stood like statues, watching as Rose knelt beside Snow, cradling the girl's head in her lap. Snow's eyes were closed. She wasn't breathing.

"We have to get the piece of apple out!" Rose said, looking up into Rapunzel's eyes. "It's poison!" Rose struggled to lift Snow's limp body. That was when Rapunzel started to move. In a flash she understood everything. Snow had been tricked.

Before she even thought about what she was doing, Rapunzel had her arms around Snow. Ella was beside her. Together the three girls got Snow to her feet and Rapunzel adjusted her arms, squeezing her fist sharply under Snow's rib cage.

Snow coughed, dislodging the tainted apple. The pale girl opened her eyes and looked at her friends, dazed. "Hi-ho," she said softly, seeming surprised to see them there. "Why, I feel a little funny."

Rapunzel, Ella, and Rose collapsed into Snow, enveloping her in a huge hug.

"Oh, Snow!" Rapunzel breathed in relief. "I think you're going to be all right."

After a few moments of relieved and nervous giggling, Rapunzel pulled out of the embrace.

"That was close," Rose said, keeping an arm around Snow.

"Rose, how did you know?" Rapunzel asked.

"I saw it all in the Hall of Mirrors," Rose said somberly. "Malodora was there, and the magic mirror, too. It was cracked, Snow."

Snow sat down on the grass with a bump. "You mean . . ."

"That apple was from Malodora? She was trying to get Snow? Right here?" Ella asked with wide eyes. "I don't believe it."

"She's jealous," Rose said sheepishly, sitting beside Snow. "And, oh, Ella! So was I! I'm sorry. I'm sorry I've been acting funny, and I'm sorry about the race. I didn't fall on purpose, but it wasn't a complete accident, either. I heard those other princesses chanting your name and . . ."

Ella didn't let Rose finish. "*You* were jealous of *me*?" She laughed, plunked down on the grass, and hugged her friend. "I'm sorry, too. I should have realized I was neglecting my real friends."

Rapunzel shook her head as she stared at the three girls on the ground. "Wow. I knew something was going on," she said. "I guess I was too wrapped up in the Games."

"I'll say," said a familiar voice behind Rapunzel. Rapunzel didn't know how long Val had been standing there. In fact, she had pretty much forgotten that they were still on the field in front of the grandstand! She was just so glad that her friends were together, and okay.

"I can't believe Malodora tried to cheat," Val said. "She's a judge!"

Grabbing Val's hand, Rapunzel pulled him down into the small circle on the grass. "Let's put this all behind us," she said somberly, using her best coaching voice. "We must stick together in the face of Grimm reality."

Val groaned. He knew Rapunzel's puns seldom traveled alone.

"We all know Malodora is far from the fairest in the land." Rapunzel kept joking, finally managing to coax a smile, then a full-fledged laugh out of Snow.

The five friends sat in a circle, oblivious to the chaos on the field. Officials were rushing to see if Snow was okay, but hadn't made it through the crowds.

Suddenly the laughing stopped. A shadow fell across the grass and Rapunzel felt instantly cold.

"Snow White," Malodora hissed. She stood over the group of friends. Hortense stood behind her, peeking around the queen's flowing purple-black robes.

The smile disappeared from Snow's face. For an instant she looked paler than Rapunzel thought possible. Then she stood and flashed a winning smile. "Oh, hello, Stepmother," she chirped. "Have you met my friends?"

Val and the girls scrambled to their feet to stand beside Snow. They bowed politely, but Malodora didn't acknowledge them. Her glare never left Snow White.

And, Rapunzel noticed proudly, Snow White never looked away or stopped smiling. The silence was interrupted when all seven dwarves finally ducked through the crowd to circle Snow.

"You were amazing," Mort chirped.

"Stupendous!" Hap added.

"Wow," Meek whispered.

"I don't think you've met my dear *family* yet, either," Snow cooed to Malodora. "That's Mort and Hap and Nod and Meek and Dim and Gruff and Wheezer."

Malodora's glossy red lips twitched. Her shoulders trembled in rage.

Snow stood still and tall, waiting for her stepmother to speak. Rapunzel thought Snow looked ready for anything.

But no one expected what happened next. The crowd parted and Lady Bathilde walked silently up behind the girls to place a hand on Snow's shoulder.

"Snow, I am so glad to see that you're all right," she said in her soft regal voice. "And Mal," she said, turning to the evil queen and speaking familiarly, "you must be so proud. Your Snow so easily captures the loyalty of her peers." Lady Bathilde smiled at Rose, Ella, Rapunzel, and Val. Rapunzel had never stood so close to the headmistress before and felt almost as if she were under a wonderful spell.

Lady Bathilde's voice alone was enough to inspire awe and royal respect as she went on. "Snow effortlessly gains the adulation of every creature around her.

As I recall, that was what you struggled with most at Princess School, was it not?"

Rapunzel's jaw dropped. Malodora went to Princess School? Looking at Snow, she saw that this was news to her, too. But instead of looking simply shocked or even angry, Snow suddenly gazed at her stepmother with *sympathy*.

Leave it to Snow to be understanding of someone so awful! Rapunzel thought. *Although*, she supposed, *I guess we all want to be liked.* Rapunzel watched Malodora's face as Lady Bathilde continued. She was striking, and would be truly gorgeous if she weren't so cruel. . . .

"Of course we are all so pleased to have Snow here at Princess School. I myself have been personally keeping an eye on her." Lady Bathilde smiled at Malodora as if she were doing the evil queen a personal favor. Malodora could only nod.

When Malodora turned to leave, she had to steady herself on Hortense's head, flattening the young witch's hat.

"You have all performed admirably today," Lady Bathilde said after Malodora had gone. "Whether we win or lose, you should be proud."

Rapunzel *was* proud, she suddenly realized. She smiled and Val elbowed her in the arm.

"Don't try to tell me you don't care if you won or lost," he said, disbelieving.

"I wouldn't say that I didn't care. . . ." Rapunzel admitted. Actually, she was dying to know!

Near the judges' stand the apples were still being counted. Rapunzel watched Vermin Twitch whisper something in Malodora's ear. Malodora smiled slightly, but her eyes narrowed before she raised her hands to silence the crowd. "It appears," she announced, "that the Apple Bob is tied. In light of this, the victory and Golden Ball will go to the Grimm School."

"Wait!" Ella shouted. Rapunzel turned to see Ella lunging for the last apple that had fallen out of Snow's mouth. It was sitting by the sidelines and hadn't been counted!

Lucinta Pintch must have spotted it at the same moment. Ella's and Lucinta's heads banged together as they grabbed for the fallen fruit. Lucinta was jabbed by Ella's tiara and Meek, who was standing nearby, shyly plucked the apple from the ground and handed it to Rapunzel.

Rapunzel marched up to Malodora and looked her in the eye. "Don't forget this one!" she said, sweet as Snow.

Chapter Twenty-one
Sweet Victory

As soon as he saw the red-and-white apple Rapunzel held, Fistius Ballus took the podium from Malodora. Rapunzel wasn't sure, but he almost seemed . . . smug. "The Apple Bob and the Maiden Games victory go to Princess School!" he proclaimed.

The field erupted into a chorus of cheers and applause. Snow felt ready to burst. She could not remember ever feeling so happy or so proud. She was proud of her school for fighting back against the Grimms. She was proud of her friends for helping her overcome her fears. And most of all she was proud of herself for finally standing up to Malodora. She knew she never could have done it before, not without her friends and not without the dwarves. And in the end she had done it with them, and for them, too. Even Lady Bathilde had been there!

Every princess in the school marched together

around the whole arena. Music played behind the procession and flower petals rained down over everything.

The Grimm witches stood under their own dark cloud, muttering and grumbling and shaking off the delicate petals as if they would be burned by them. Snow *almost* felt bad for the witches. Almost.

After the procession, Snow and Rose settled into the bleachers. With a minimum of fanfare Ella returned her tiara, holding out a delicate but calloused hand to quiet the applause. When she joined her friends in the stands, the three girls grinned as they watched Rapunzel take the stage with the other Princess School captains for the presentation of the Golden Ball.

Vermin and Fistius held the orb aloft. Glowing almost magically in the slanted sunlight, it was one of the prettiest things Snow had ever seen.

"It gives me great pleasure to award the Golden Ball to the winner of the Maiden Games — Princess School!" Fistius announced. Vermin twitched, and together they handed the ball to Rapunzel, who was first in line for the Princess team.

In the stands Snow leaped to her feet. She, Ella, and Rose jumped and cheered as Rapunzel held the ball over her head. It almost looked like an egg in her nest of hair.

Snow watched Rapunzel search for her friends in the grandstand, then looked at each one of them and lifted the ball higher before passing it to the Sash captain, who passed it to the Robe captain, who finally handed it to the Crown captain.

Snow sat back down but kept her eyes on Rapunzel. Rapunzel, though, was looking at someone else. She was watching Val, and her victory smile was fading. Snow followed Rapunzel's gaze to Val, then followed Val's gaze . . . to Rose. Feeling a familiar twinge in her stomach, Snow swallowed hard and looked away. She'd had enough of jealousy, and nothing was going to ruin her mood.

The sun was beginning to set as the presentation ceremony ended. The princesses politely waved goodbye to the Grimm witches as they skulked into the forest with their brooms between their legs. It was clear the Grimms would be counting the seconds until the next Maiden Games and their chance for revenge. But they could not change the fact that Princess School had won, fair and square. Malodora led the Grimm group out without a backward glance.

"Who wants to come to the cottage for supper?" Snow asked, clapping her hands together when Rapunzel had rejoined the group.

"What a wonderful idea!" Mort said as he jumped off the last grandstand seat.

"Jolly good," said Hap.

"Nobody will miss me at the tower." Rapunzel shrugged.

"I think it's worth a few extra chores." Ella grinned.

"Just a moment. I have to get permission." Rose hurried to the edge of the field where carriages and coaches were starting to line up. She poked her head inside one and a few minutes later she was back with seven fairies fluttering all around her face, putting out a soft glow. "I can go if I take my bodyguards." She smiled and tilted her head toward the fairies.

"Ooh, they're lovely," Snow cooed. "We can collect some dew and nectar for them on the way."

The walk to the cottage felt like an extension of the victory procession. The dwarves hummed, the fairies made tiny chiming sounds, and the girls recalled the most exciting moments of the day as they made their way through the darkening forest. The last rays of pink sun glinted on the damp leaves, and the tree branches made lacy patterns on the sunset sky.

The party at the cottage was no less glorious. The food was a little strange (the dwarves cooked), but the music was wonderful and Rose's fairies even provided some fireworks.

It was late when Snow finally hugged her friends good-bye. Sleepily she walked up the stairs to her room. Then with a yawn she fell into the bed the dwarves had carved just for her. That night she slept soundly with a small smile on her face and had nothing but sweet dreams.

The
Princess School

Book Three
Let Down Your Hair
by Jane B. Mason and Sarah Hines Stephens

Rapunzel and Val have been best friends
for years. She's always been able to count
on him to help her through a tangle. But
lately, Val hasn't been paying much attention
to Rapunzel — he's too busy fawning over
Rose. Rapunzel could really use Val and her
other friends right now. Madame Gothel, the
witch who keeps Rapunzel locked in the tower,
just discovered that she has been climbing out
to attend Princess School. Madame Gothel is
furious — and determined to keep Rapunzel
from escaping again. Will Rapunzel lose her
friends, Princess School, and her freedom all
at once —
or is there a way to get the
witch out of her hair?

■SCHOLASTIC

Ella. Snow. Rapunzel. Rose.
Four friends who wait for no prince.

from best-selling authors
Jane B. Mason and Sarah Hines Stephens

With her feet bare (those glass slippers don't fit), and her second-hand gown splattered with mud (thanks, evil stepsisters), Ella's first day of Princess School is off to a lousy start. Then she meets silly Snow, adventurous Rapunzel, and beautiful, sheltered Rose. Ella's new friends make Princess School bearable—even fun. But can they help Ella stand up to her horrible steps in time for the Coronation Ball?

In stores this May!

PS1T

More Series You'll Fall in Love With

Heartland™

Nestled in the foothills of Virginia, there's a place where horses come when they are hurt. Amy, Ty, and everyone at Heartland work together to heal the horses—and form lasting bonds that will touch your heart.

In a family of superstars, it's hard to stand out. But Abby is about to surprise her friends, her family, and most of all, herself!

The AMAZING DAYS of ABBY HAYES®

Jody is about to begin a dream vacation on the wide open sea, traveling to new places and helping her parents with their dolphin research.

You can tag along with

Dolphin Diaries

■ SCHOLASTIC

www.scholastic.com/books

GIRLT1